GET IN THE GAME

STAR STRIKER

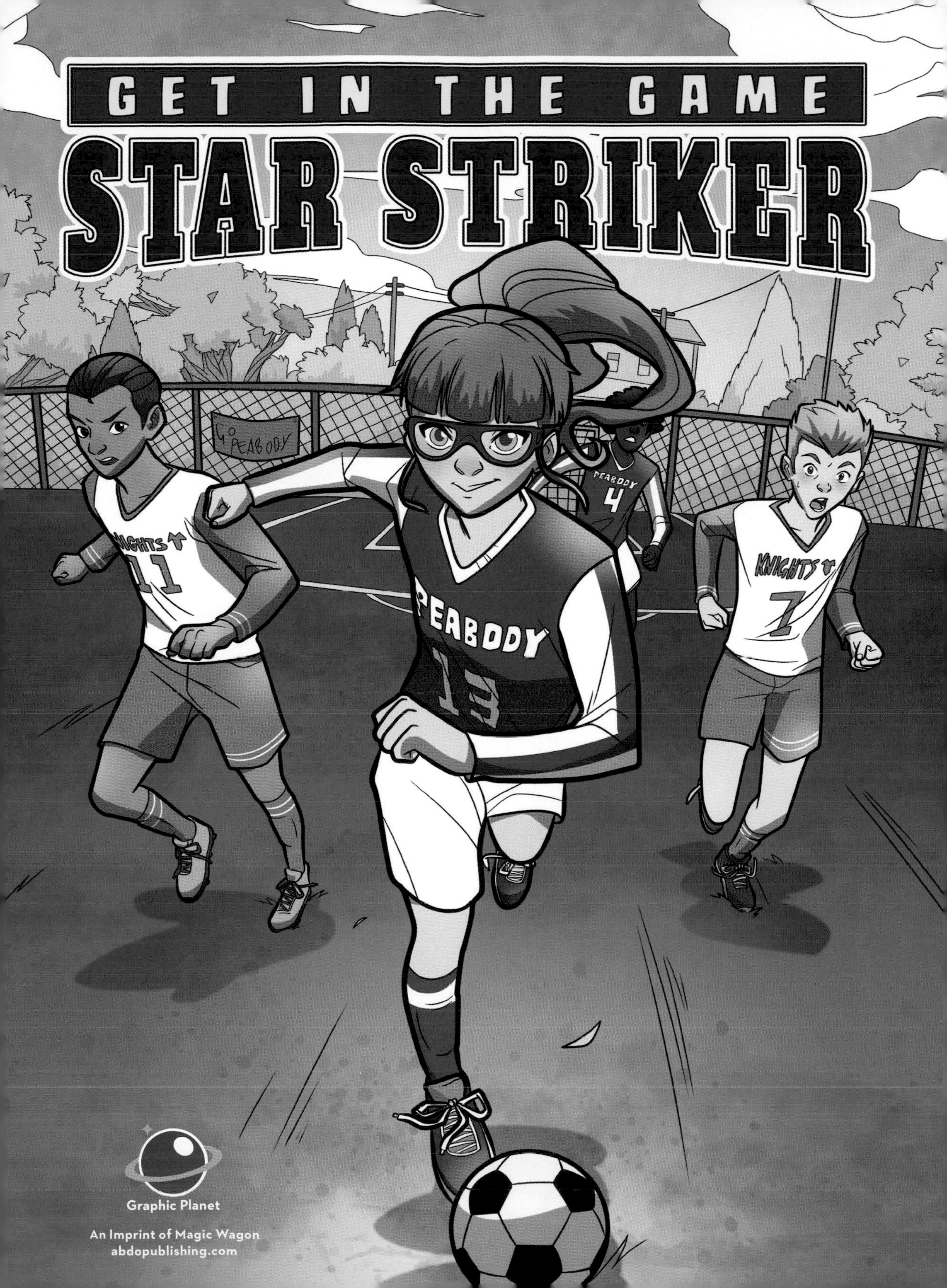
GO PEABODY
KNIGHTS 11
PEABODY 4
PEABODY 13
KNIGHTS 7

Graphic Planet
An Imprint of Magic Wagon
abdopublishing.com

abdopublishing.com

Published by Magic Wagon, a division of ABDO, PO Box 398166, Minneapolis, Minnesota 55439.
Copyright © 2019 by Abdo Consulting Group, Inc. International copyrights reserved in all countries.
No part of this book may be reproduced in any form without written permission from the publisher.
Graphic Planet™ is a trademark and logo of Magic Wagon.

Printed in the United States of America, North Mankato, Minnesota.
052018
092018

THIS BOOK CONTAINS RECYCLED MATERIALS

Written by Bill Yu
Illustrated by Renato Siragusa
Colored by Tiziana Musmeci
Lettered by Kathryn S. Renta
Card Illustrations by Emanuele Cardillo and Gabriele Cracolici (Grafimated)
Layout and design by Pejee Calanog of Glass House Graphics and Christina Doffing of ABDO
Editorial supervision by David Campiti and Salvatore Di Marco (Grafimated Cartoon)
Edited by Salvatore Di Marco and Giovanni Spadaro (Grafimated Cartoon)
Packaged by Glass House Graphics
Art Directed by Candice Keimig
Editorial Support by Tamara L. Britton

Library of Congress Control Number: 2018932636

Publisher's Cataloging-in-Publication Data

Names: Yu, Bill, author. | Siragusa, Renato, illustrator.
Title: Star striker / by Bill Yu; illustrated by Renato Siragusa.
Description: Minneapolis, Minnesota : Magic Wagon, 2019. | Series: Get in the game
Summary: Katie Flanagan was a star striker on her old school's soccer team. But at Peabody, there is no
    girls' soccer team. The school district allows Katie to try out for the boys' team. Having a girl play on
    the boys' team causes some conflict. Can Katie overcome these barriers?
Identifiers: ISBN 9781532132971 (lib.bdg.) | ISBN 9781532133114 (ebook) |
    ISBN 9781532133183 (Read-to-me ebook)
Subjects: LCSH: Soccer--Juvenile fiction. | School sports for girls--Juvenile fiction. | Sex discrimination in
    sports--Juvenile fiction. | Self-reliance in adolescence--Juvenile fiction. | Graphic novels--Juvenile
    fiction.
Classification: DDC 741.5--dc23

CONTENTS

STAR STRIKER

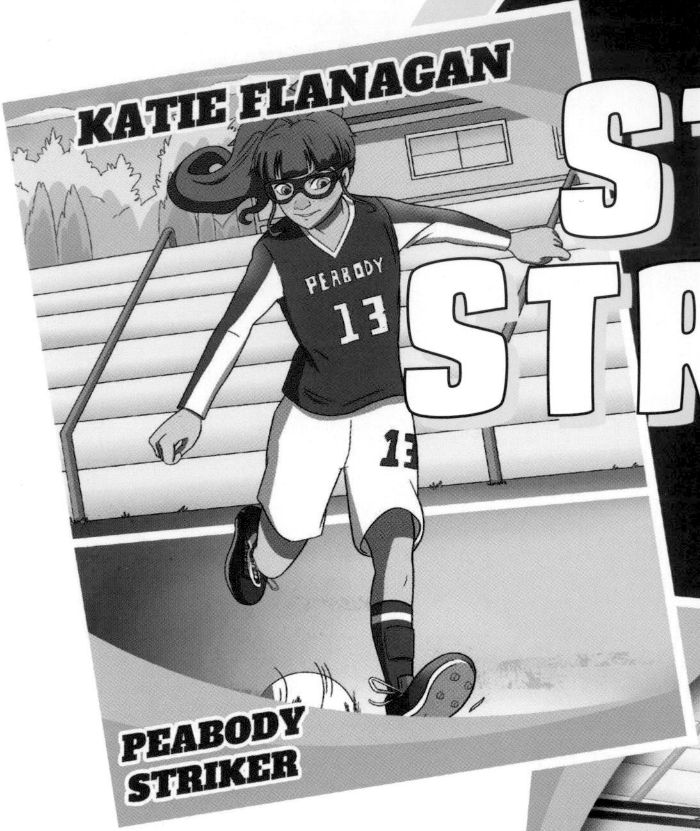
KATIE FLANAGAN
PEABODY
13
PEABODY STRIKER

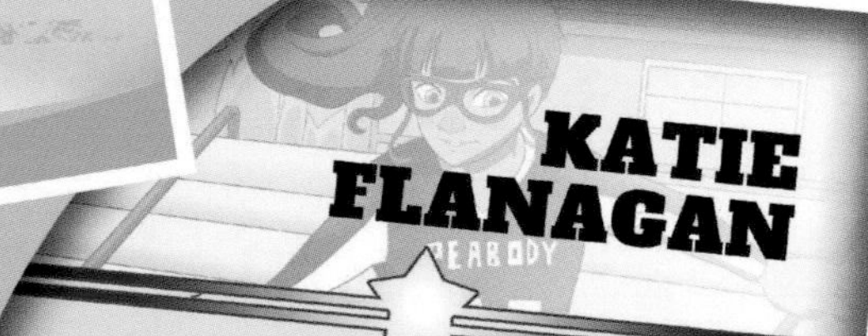
KATIE FLANAGAN
PEABODY

Katie Flanagan, Striker #13

Katie Flanagan is a striker who can run with speed and shoot with accuracy. As a new arrival to the community, great things are hoped for with Peabody's newest soccer transfer after two fantastic seasons at Mackenzie Middle school.

RECORD

GAMES	GOALS	SHOTS	SHOTS ON GOAL	ASSISTS	YELLOW CARDS	RED CARDS
16	32	40	38	15	2	0

Note: statistics are from last year's season at Mackenzie MS

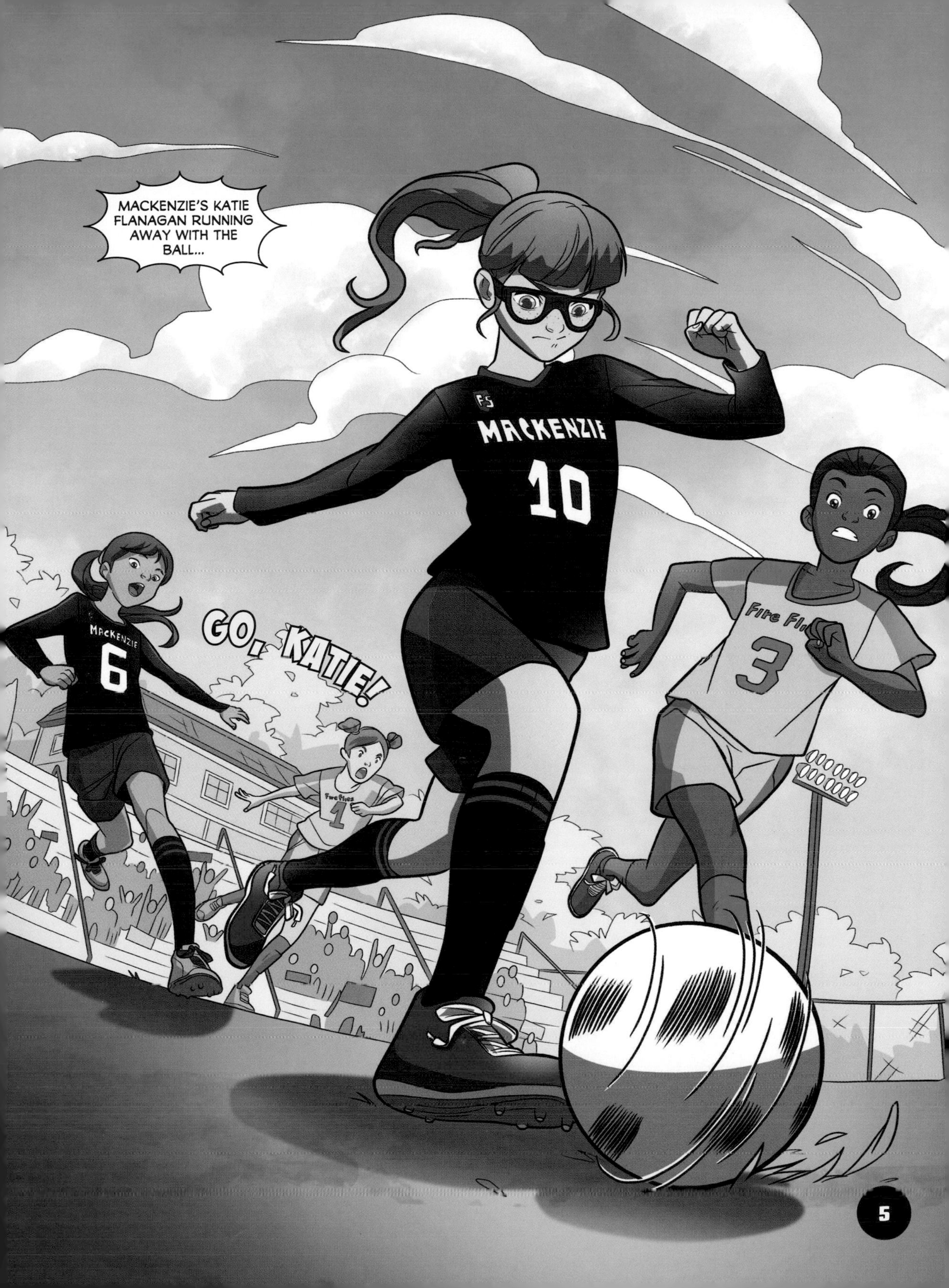
MACKENZIE'S KATIE FLANAGAN RUNNING AWAY WITH THE BALL...
GO, KATIE!
MACKENZIE
10
MACKENZIE
6
Fire Flies
1
Fire Fli
3

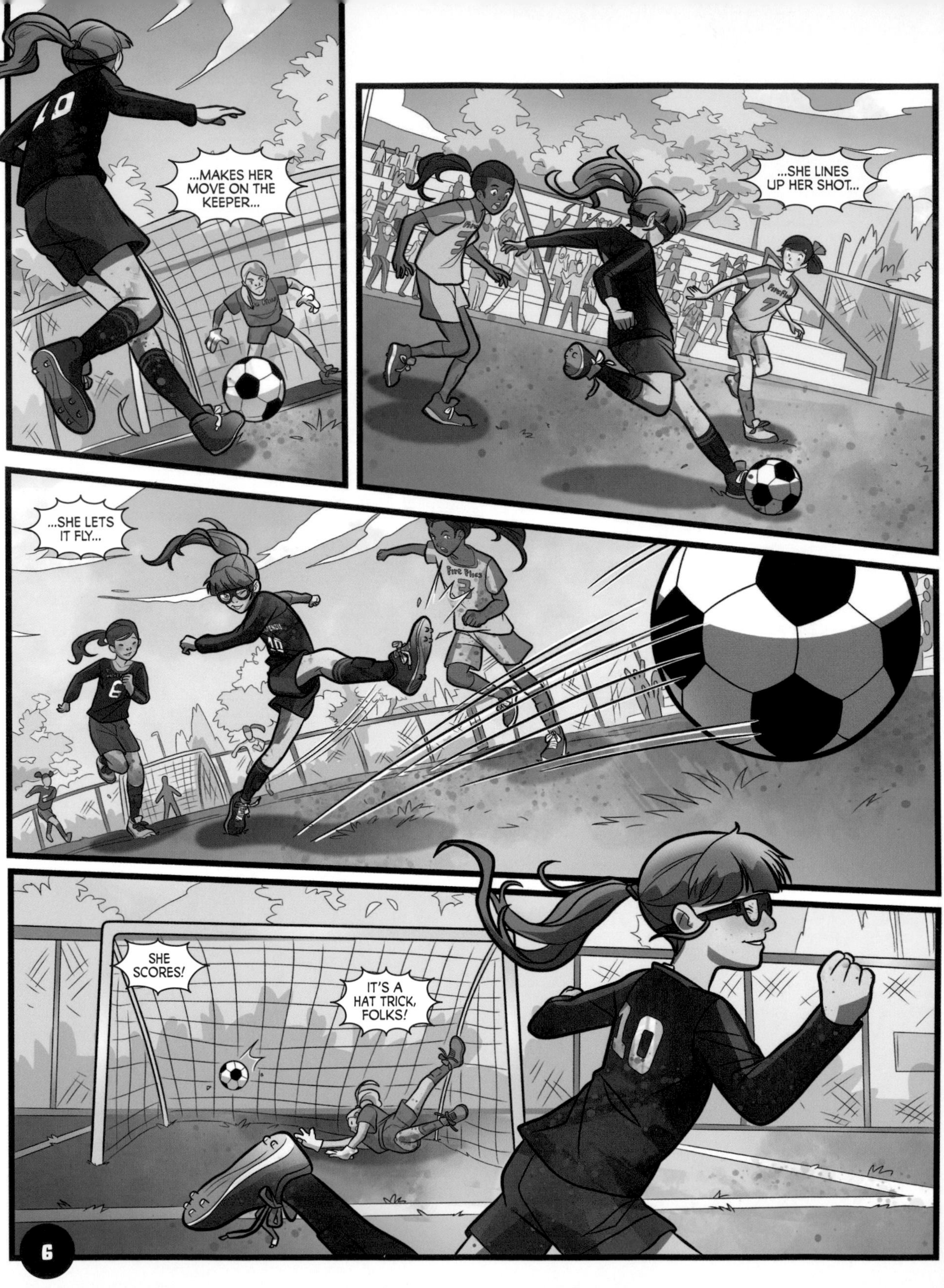
...MAKES HER MOVE ON THE KEEPER...
...SHE LINES UP HER SHOT...
...SHE LETS IT FLY...
SHE SCORES!
IT'S A HAT TRICK, FOLKS!

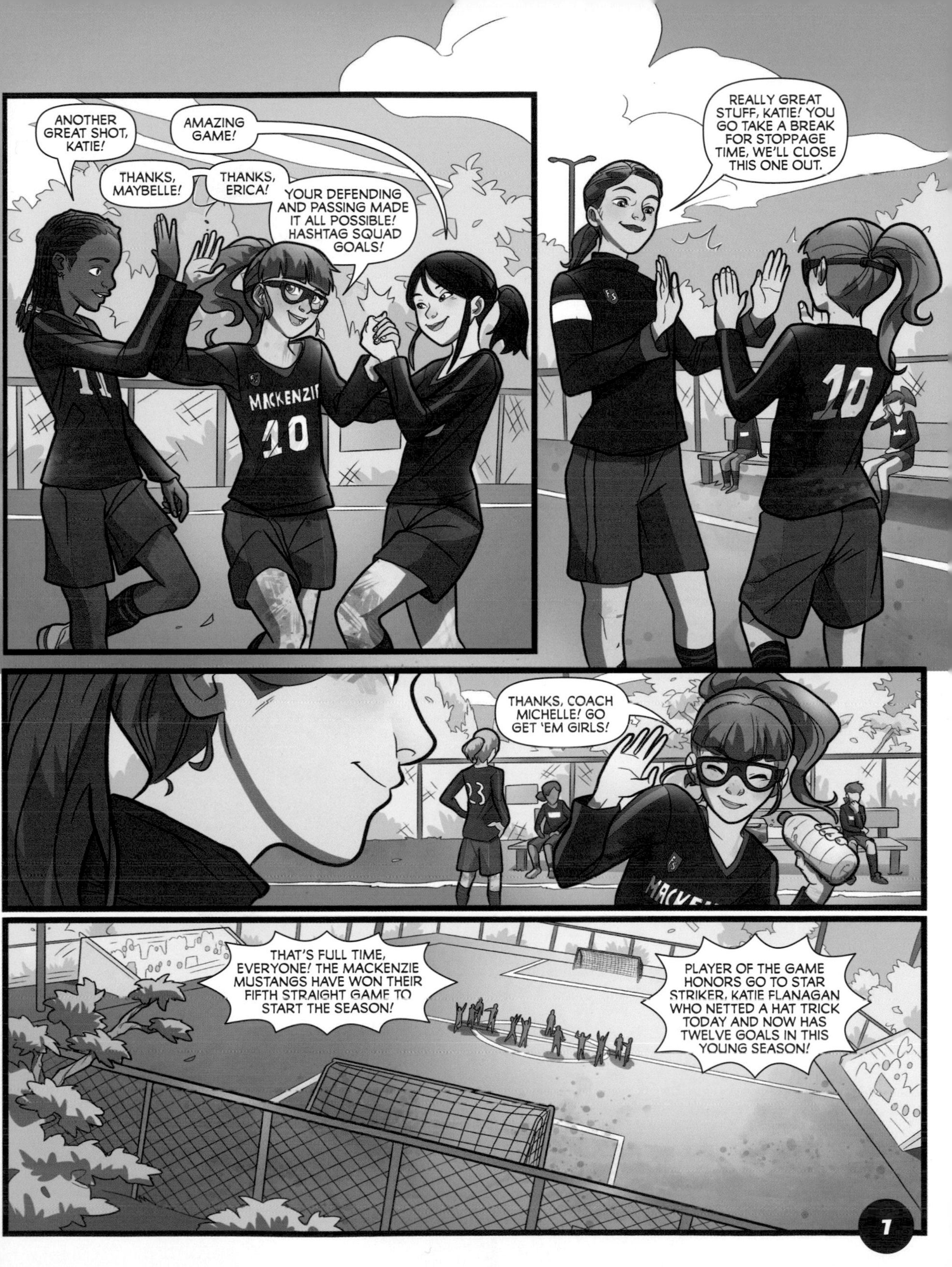
ANOTHER GREAT SHOT, KATIE!
AMAZING GAME!
THANKS, MAYBELLE!
THANKS, ERICA!
YOUR DEFENDING AND PASSING MADE IT ALL POSSIBLE! HASHTAG SQUAD GOALS!
MACKENZIE
10
11
REALLY GREAT STUFF, KATIE! YOU GO TAKE A BREAK FOR STOPPAGE TIME, WE'LL CLOSE THIS ONE OUT.
10
THANKS, COACH MICHELLE! GO GET 'EM GIRLS!
23
THAT'S FULL TIME, EVERYONE! THE MACKENZIE MUSTANGS HAVE WON THEIR FIFTH STRAIGHT GAME TO START THE SEASON!
PLAYER OF THE GAME HONORS GO TO STAR STRIKER, KATIE FLANAGAN WHO NETTED A HAT TRICK TODAY AND NOW HAS TWELVE GOALS IN THIS YOUNG SEASON!

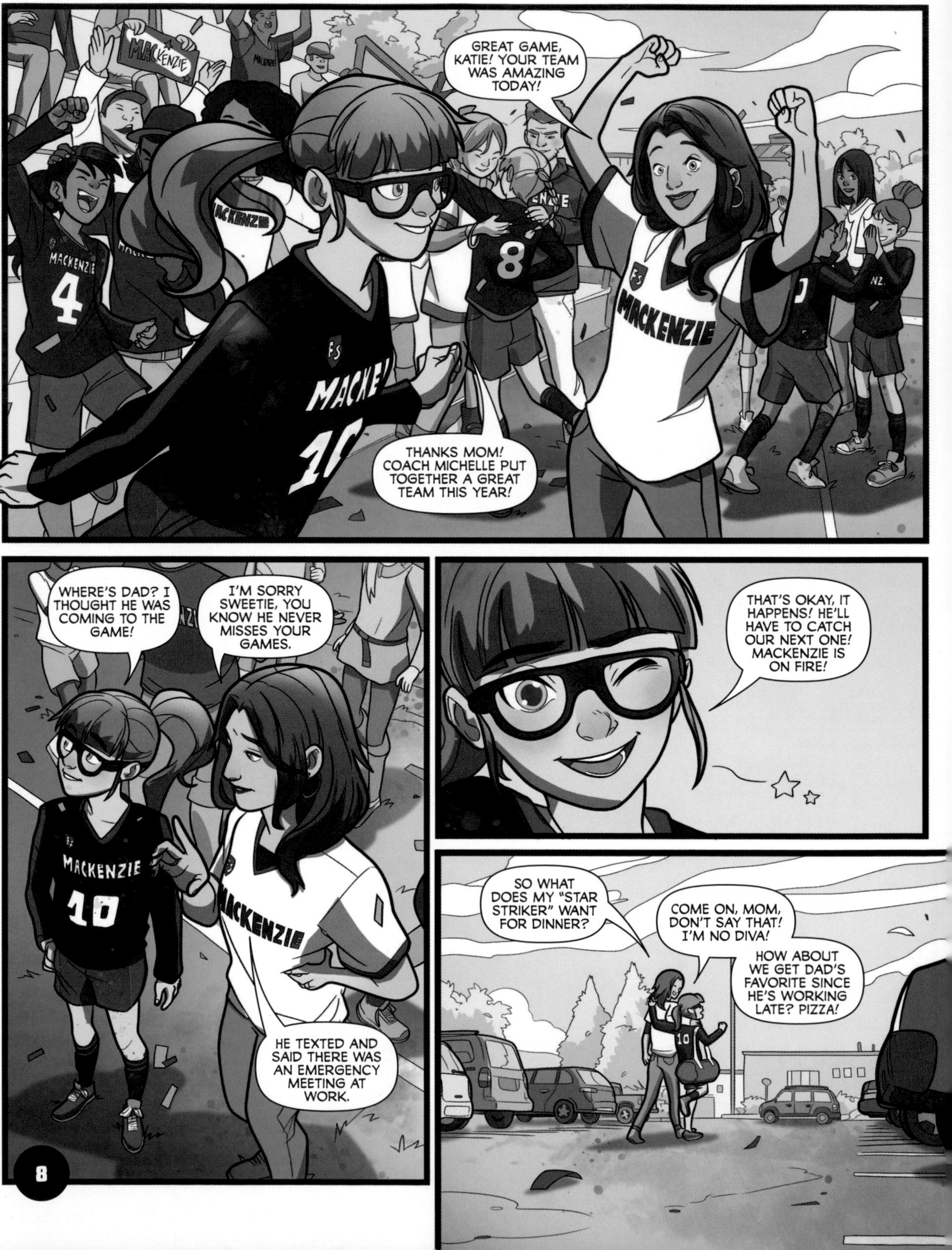
GREAT GAME, KATIE! YOUR TEAM WAS AMAZING TODAY!
THANKS MOM! COACH MICHELLE PUT TOGETHER A GREAT TEAM THIS YEAR!
WHERE'S DAD? I THOUGHT HE WAS COMING TO THE GAME!
I'M SORRY SWEETIE, YOU KNOW HE NEVER MISSES YOUR GAMES.
HE TEXTED AND SAID THERE WAS AN EMERGENCY MEETING AT WORK.
THAT'S OKAY, IT HAPPENS! HE'LL HAVE TO CATCH OUR NEXT ONE! MACKENZIE IS ON FIRE!
SO WHAT DOES MY "STAR STRIKER" WANT FOR DINNER?
COME ON, MOM, DON'T SAY THAT! I'M NO DIVA!
HOW ABOUT WE GET DAD'S FAVORITE SINCE HE'S WORKING LATE? PIZZA!

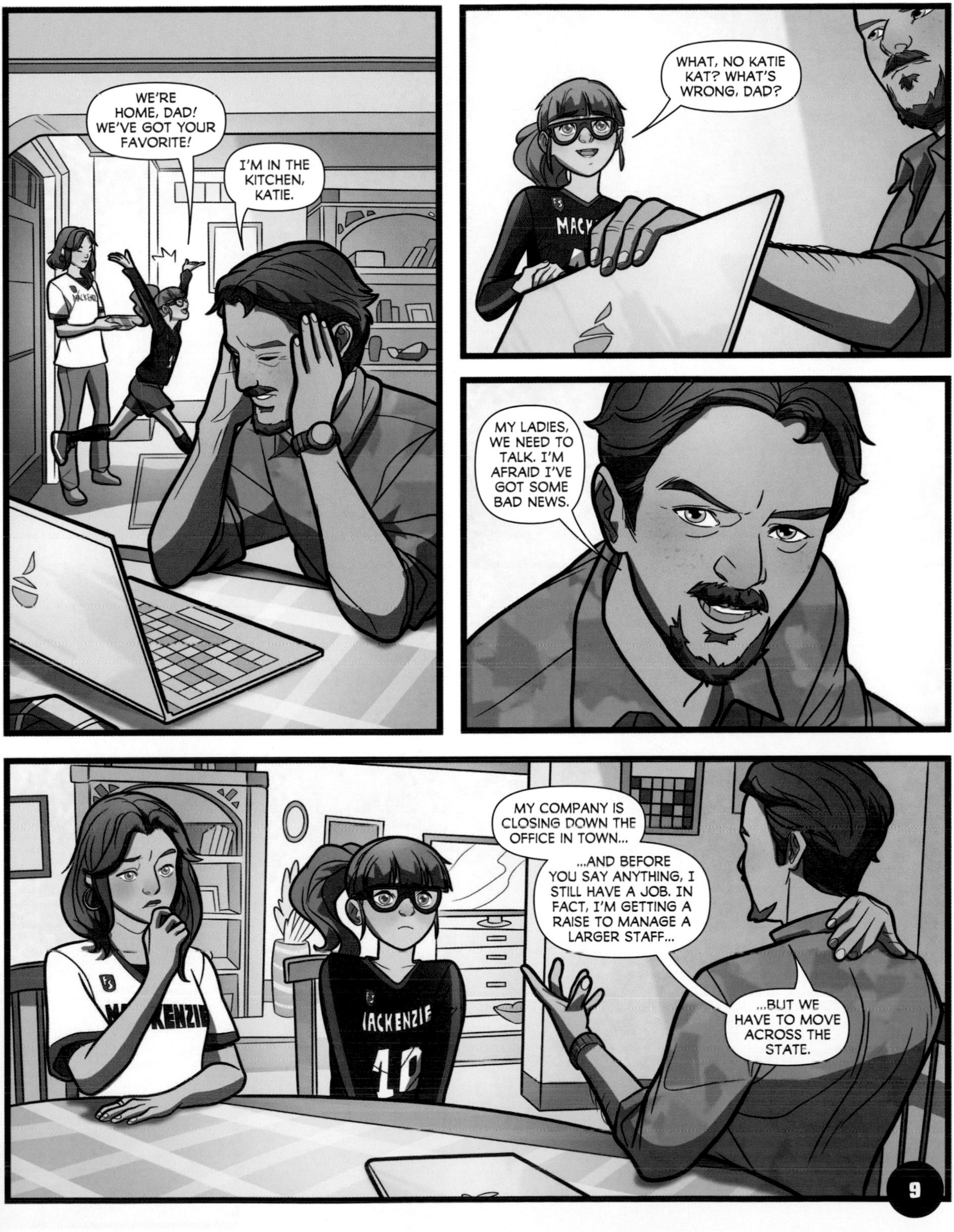
WE'RE HOME, DAD! WE'VE GOT YOUR FAVORITE!
I'M IN THE KITCHEN, KATIE.
WHAT, NO KATIE KAT? WHAT'S WRONG, DAD?
MY LADIES, WE NEED TO TALK. I'M AFRAID I'VE GOT SOME BAD NEWS.
MY COMPANY IS CLOSING DOWN THE OFFICE IN TOWN...
...AND BEFORE YOU SAY ANYTHING, I STILL HAVE A JOB. IN FACT, I'M GETTING A RAISE TO MANAGE A LARGER STAFF...
...BUT WE HAVE TO MOVE ACROSS THE STATE.

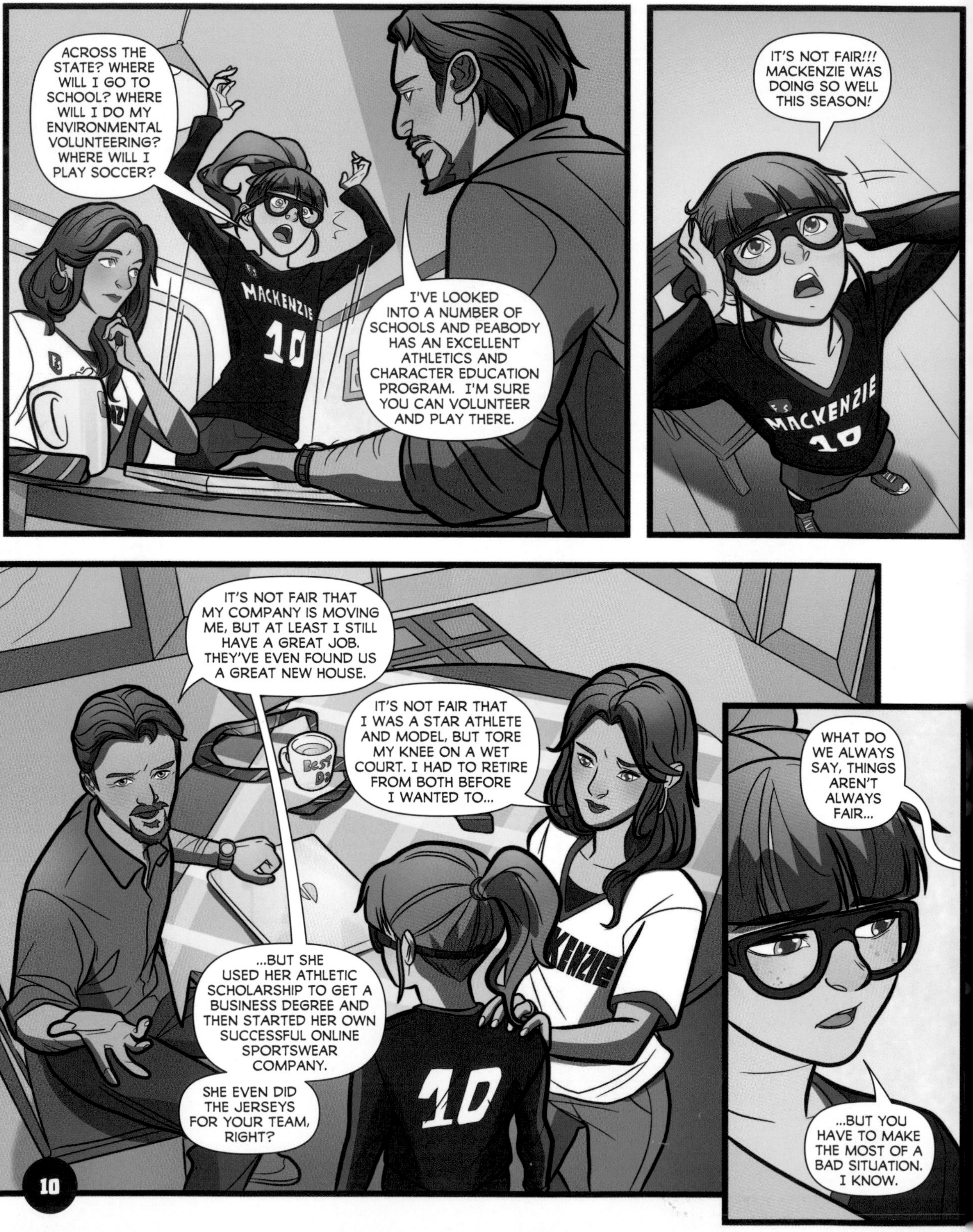
ACROSS THE STATE? WHERE WILL I GO TO SCHOOL? WHERE WILL I DO MY ENVIRONMENTAL VOLUNTEERING? WHERE WILL I PLAY SOCCER?
I'VE LOOKED INTO A NUMBER OF SCHOOLS AND PEABODY HAS AN EXCELLENT ATHLETICS AND CHARACTER EDUCATION PROGRAM. I'M SURE YOU CAN VOLUNTEER AND PLAY THERE.
IT'S NOT FAIR!!! MACKENZIE WAS DOING SO WELL THIS SEASON!
IT'S NOT FAIR THAT MY COMPANY IS MOVING ME, BUT AT LEAST I STILL HAVE A GREAT JOB. THEY'VE EVEN FOUND US A GREAT NEW HOUSE.
IT'S NOT FAIR THAT I WAS A STAR ATHLETE AND MODEL, BUT TORE MY KNEE ON A WET COURT. I HAD TO RETIRE FROM BOTH BEFORE I WANTED TO...
...BUT SHE USED HER ATHLETIC SCHOLARSHIP TO GET A BUSINESS DEGREE AND THEN STARTED HER OWN SUCCESSFUL ONLINE SPORTSWEAR COMPANY.
SHE EVEN DID THE JERSEYS FOR YOUR TEAM, RIGHT?
WHAT DO WE ALWAYS SAY, THINGS AREN'T ALWAYS FAIR...
...BUT YOU HAVE TO MAKE THE MOST OF A BAD SITUATION. I KNOW.

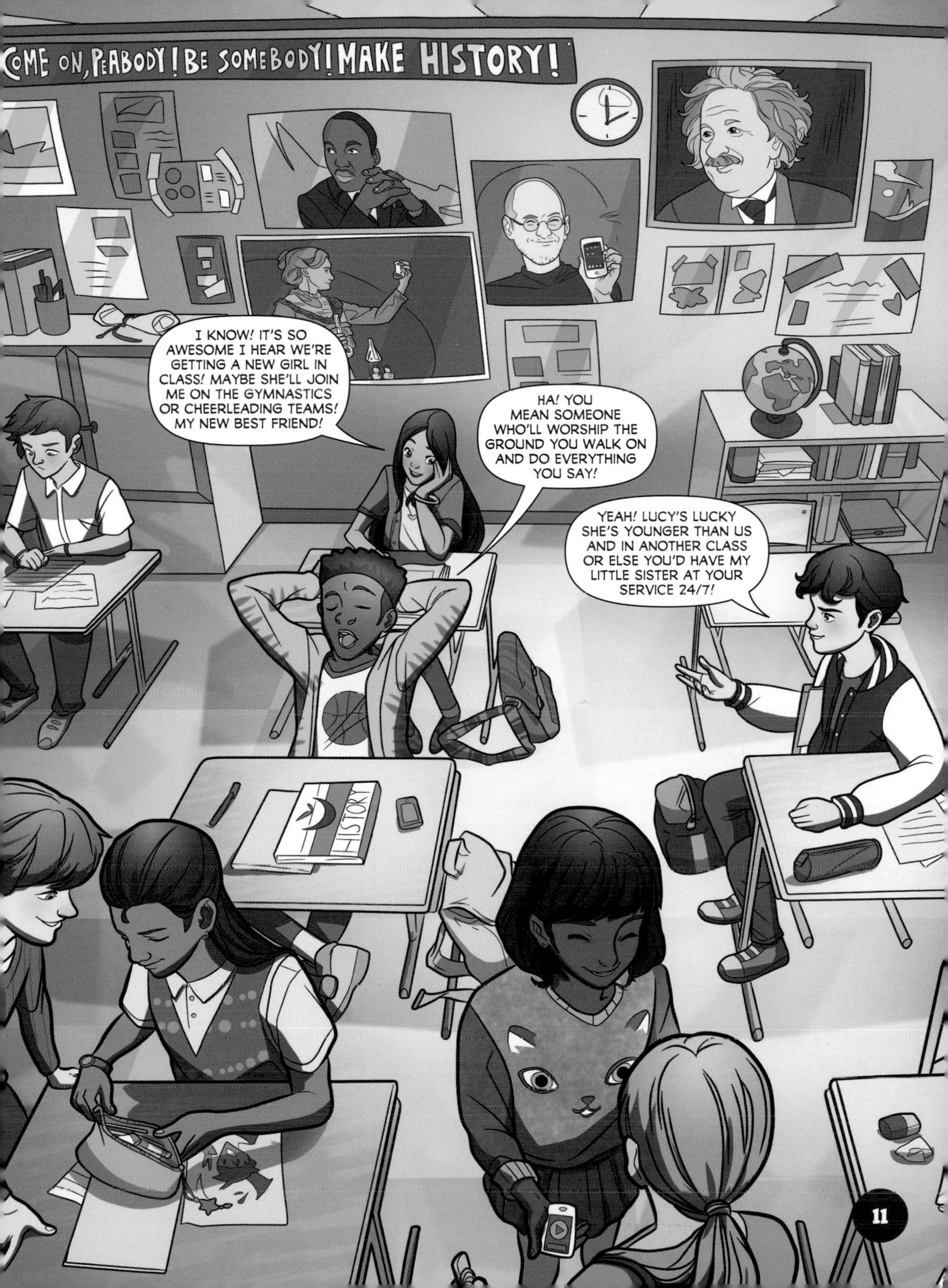
COME ON, PEABODY! BE SOMEBODY! MAKE HISTORY!
I KNOW! IT'S SO AWESOME I HEAR WE'RE GETTING A NEW GIRL IN CLASS! MAYBE SHE'LL JOIN ME ON THE GYMNASTICS OR CHEERLEADING TEAMS! MY NEW BEST FRIEND!
HA! YOU MEAN SOMEONE WHO'LL WORSHIP THE GROUND YOU WALK ON AND DO EVERYTHING YOU SAY!
YEAH! LUCY'S LUCKY SHE'S YOUNGER THAN US AND IN ANOTHER CLASS OR ELSE YOU'D HAVE MY LITTLE SISTER AT YOUR SERVICE 24/7!
HISTORY

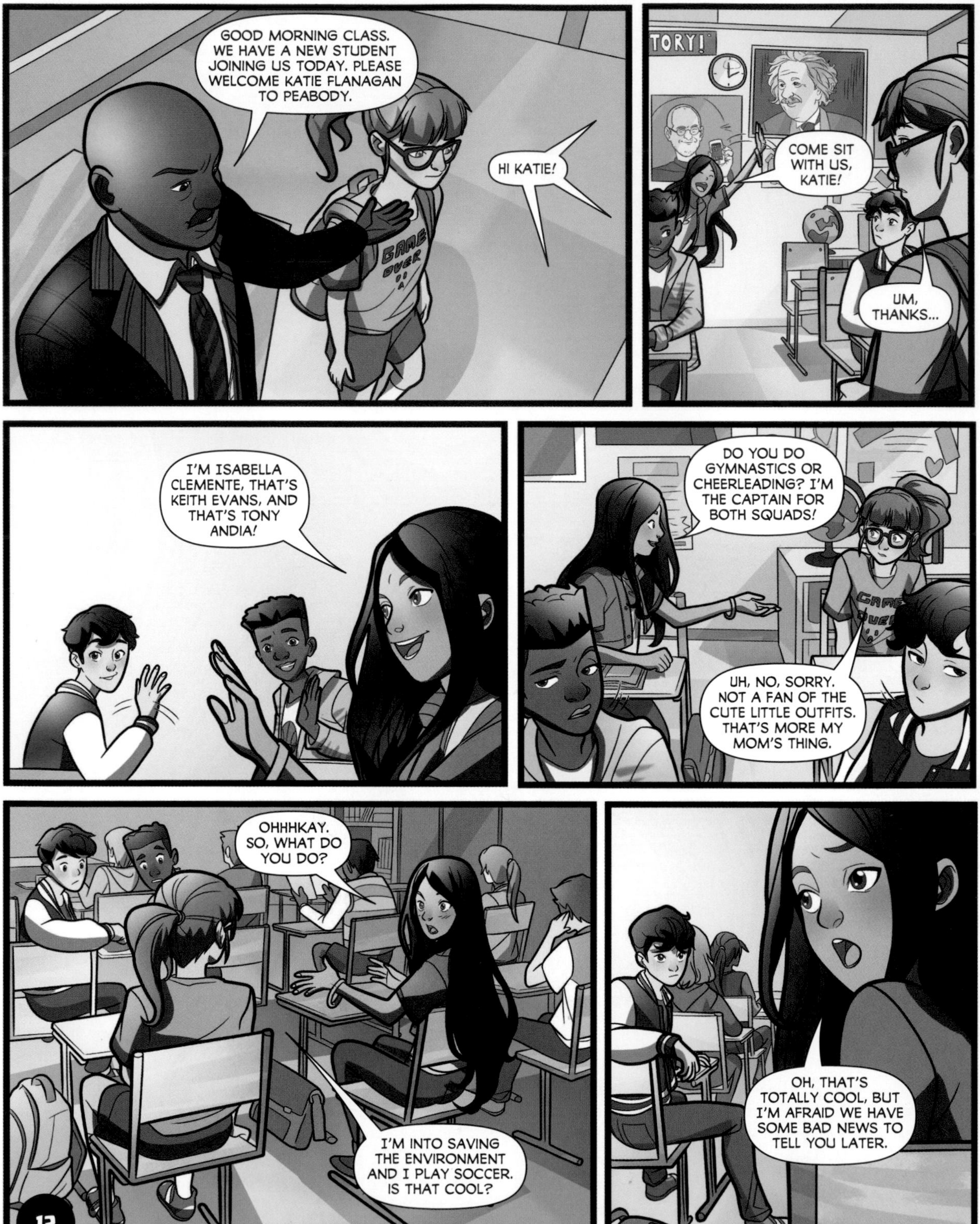
TORY!
GOOD MORNING CLASS. WE HAVE A NEW STUDENT JOINING US TODAY. PLEASE WELCOME KATIE FLANAGAN TO PEABODY.
GAME OVER
HI KATIE!
COME SIT WITH US, KATIE!
UM, THANKS...
I'M ISABELLA CLEMENTE, THAT'S KEITH EVANS, AND THAT'S TONY ANDIA!
DO YOU DO GYMNASTICS OR CHEERLEADING? I'M THE CAPTAIN FOR BOTH SQUADS!
UH, NO, SORRY. NOT A FAN OF THE CUTE LITTLE OUTFITS. THAT'S MORE MY MOM'S THING.
OHHHKAY. SO, WHAT DO YOU DO?
I'M INTO SAVING THE ENVIRONMENT AND I PLAY SOCCER. IS THAT COOL?
OH, THAT'S TOTALLY COOL, BUT I'M AFRAID WE HAVE SOME BAD NEWS TO TELL YOU LATER.

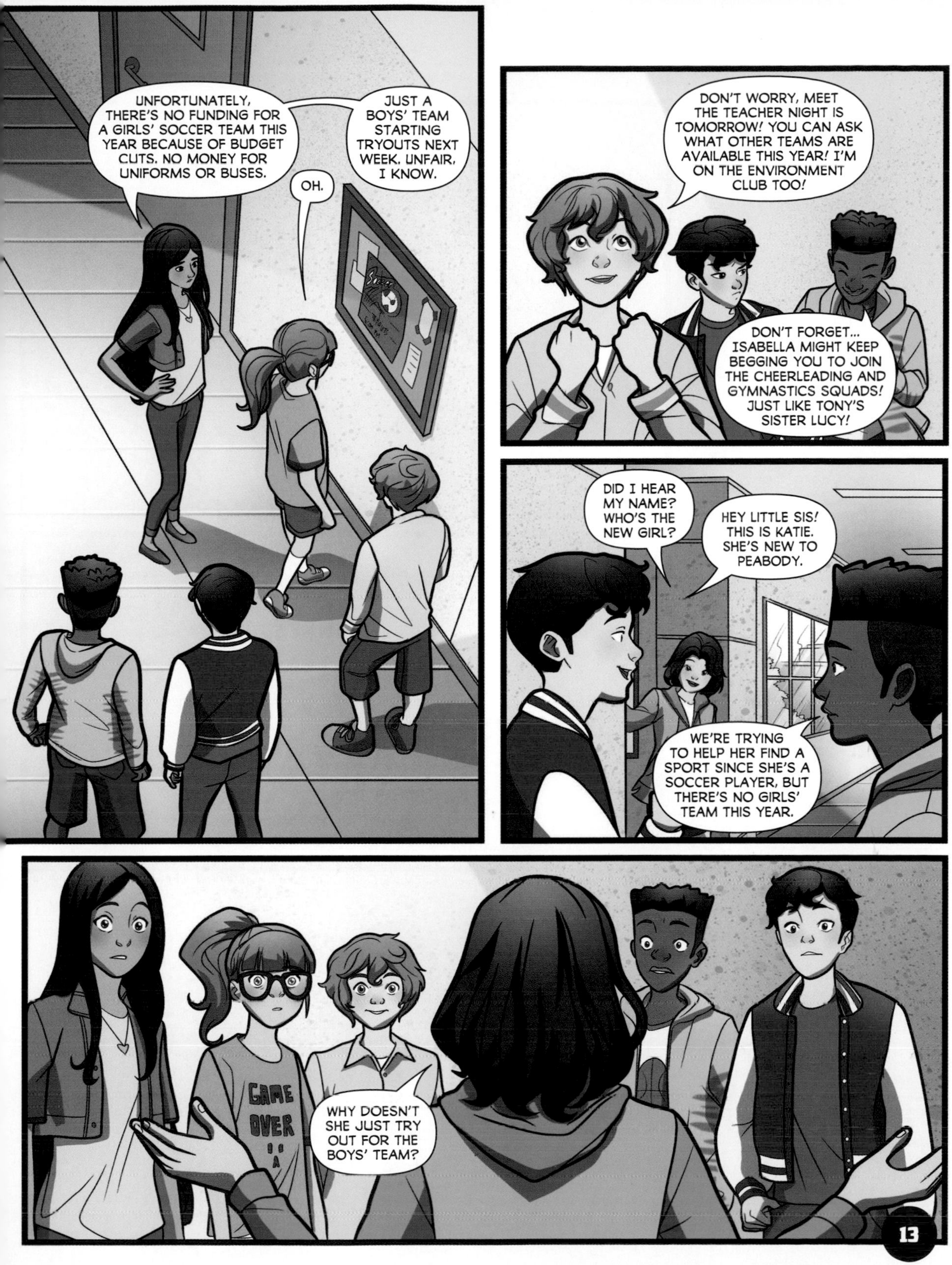

UNFORTUNATELY, THERE'S NO FUNDING FOR A GIRLS' SOCCER TEAM THIS YEAR BECAUSE OF BUDGET CUTS. NO MONEY FOR UNIFORMS OR BUSES.
JUST A BOYS' TEAM STARTING TRYOUTS NEXT WEEK. UNFAIR, I KNOW.
OH.
DON'T WORRY, MEET THE TEACHER NIGHT IS TOMORROW! YOU CAN ASK WHAT OTHER TEAMS ARE AVAILABLE THIS YEAR! I'M ON THE ENVIRONMENT CLUB TOO!
DON'T FORGET... ISABELLA MIGHT KEEP BEGGING YOU TO JOIN THE CHEERLEADING AND GYMNASTICS SQUADS! JUST LIKE TONY'S SISTER LUCY!
DID I HEAR MY NAME? WHO'S THE NEW GIRL?
HEY LITTLE SIS! THIS IS KATIE. SHE'S NEW TO PEABODY.
WE'RE TRYING TO HELP HER FIND A SPORT SINCE SHE'S A SOCCER PLAYER, BUT THERE'S NO GIRLS' TEAM THIS YEAR.
GAME OVER
WHY DOESN'T SHE JUST TRY OUT FOR THE BOYS' TEAM?

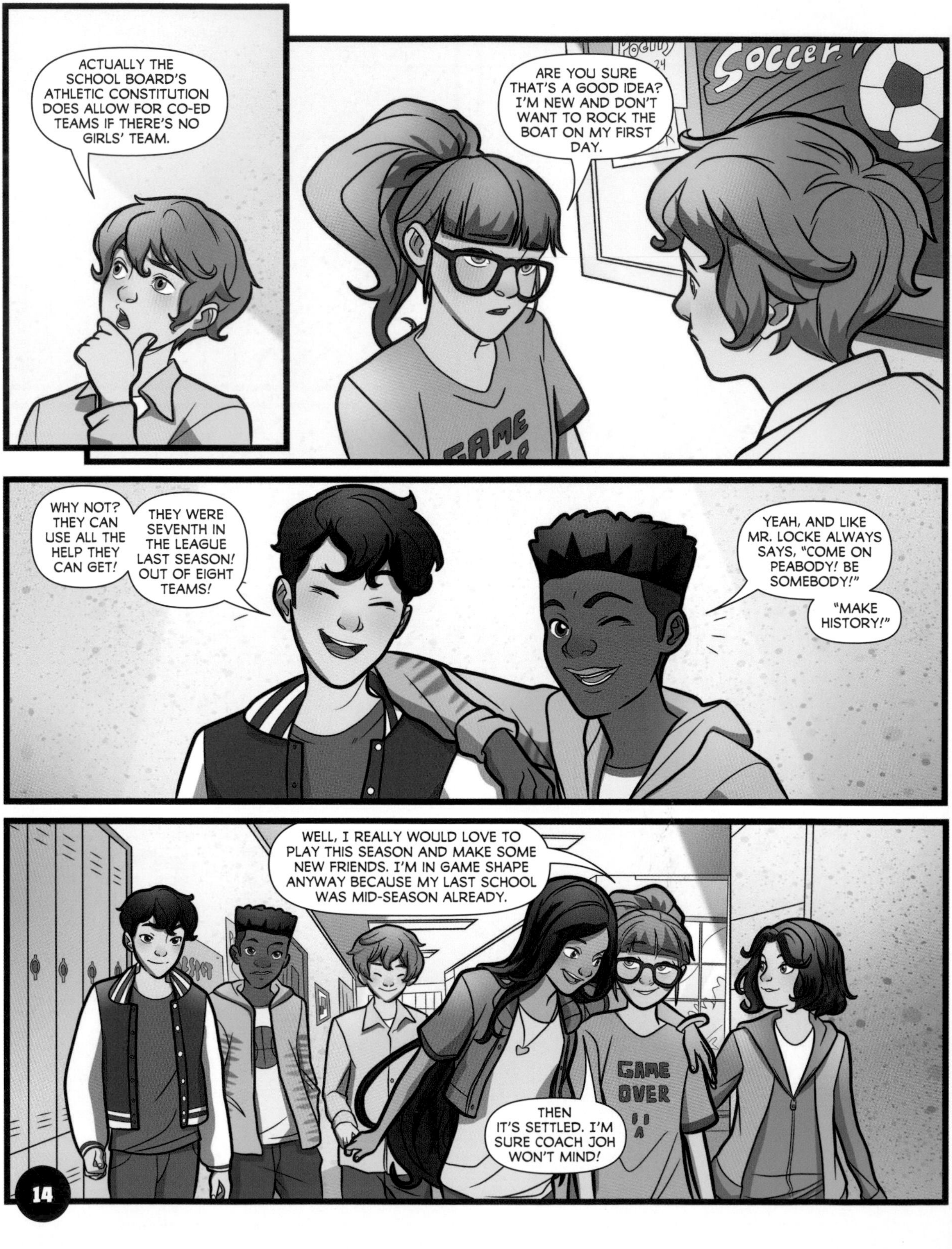
ACTUALLY THE SCHOOL BOARD'S ATHLETIC CONSTITUTION DOES ALLOW FOR CO-ED TEAMS IF THERE'S NO GIRLS' TEAM.
ARE YOU SURE THAT'S A GOOD IDEA? I'M NEW AND DON'T WANT TO ROCK THE BOAT ON MY FIRST DAY.
Soccer
WHY NOT? THEY CAN USE ALL THE HELP THEY CAN GET!
THEY WERE SEVENTH IN THE LEAGUE LAST SEASON! OUT OF EIGHT TEAMS!
YEAH, AND LIKE MR. LOCKE ALWAYS SAYS, "COME ON PEABODY! BE SOMEBODY!"
"MAKE HISTORY!"
WELL, I REALLY WOULD LOVE TO PLAY THIS SEASON AND MAKE SOME NEW FRIENDS. I'M IN GAME SHAPE ANYWAY BECAUSE MY LAST SCHOOL WAS MID-SEASON ALREADY.
GAME OVER
THEN IT'S SETTLED. I'M SURE COACH JOH WON'T MIND!

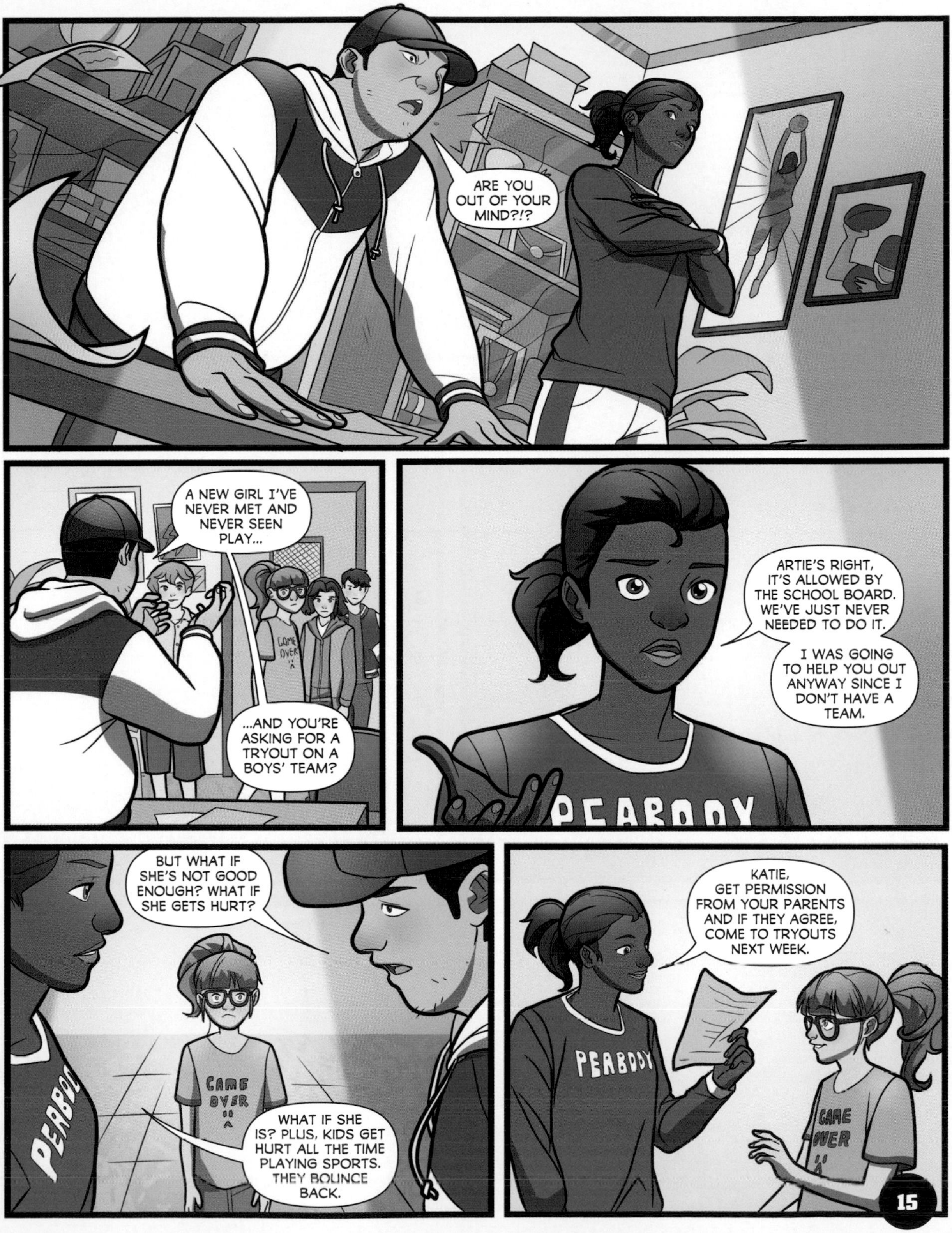
ARE YOU OUT OF YOUR MIND?!?
A NEW GIRL I'VE NEVER MET AND NEVER SEEN PLAY...
...AND YOU'RE ASKING FOR A TRYOUT ON A BOYS' TEAM?
GAME OVER
ARTIE'S RIGHT, IT'S ALLOWED BY THE SCHOOL BOARD. WE'VE JUST NEVER NEEDED TO DO IT.
I WAS GOING TO HELP YOU OUT ANYWAY SINCE I DON'T HAVE A TEAM.
PEABODY
BUT WHAT IF SHE'S NOT GOOD ENOUGH? WHAT IF SHE GETS HURT?
WHAT IF SHE IS? PLUS, KIDS GET HURT ALL THE TIME PLAYING SPORTS. THEY BOUNCE BACK.
GAME OVER
KATIE, GET PERMISSION FROM YOUR PARENTS AND IF THEY AGREE, COME TO TRYOUTS NEXT WEEK.
PEABODY
GAME OVER

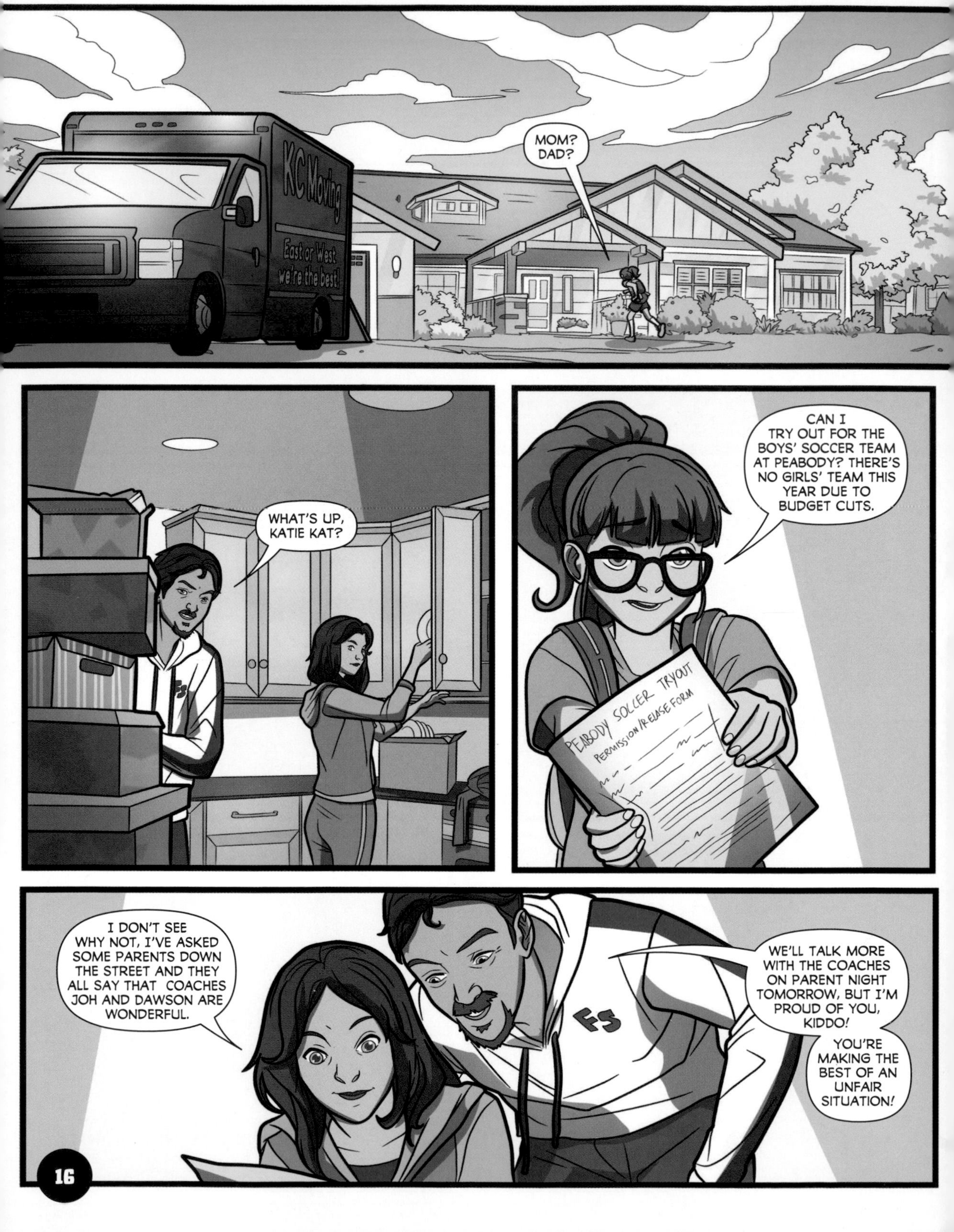
KC Moving
East or West we're the best!
MOM? DAD?
WHAT'S UP, KATIE KAT?
CAN I TRY OUT FOR THE BOYS' SOCCER TEAM AT PEABODY? THERE'S NO GIRLS' TEAM THIS YEAR DUE TO BUDGET CUTS.
PEABODY SOCCER TRYOUT
PERMISSION/RELEASE FORM
I DON'T SEE WHY NOT, I'VE ASKED SOME PARENTS DOWN THE STREET AND THEY ALL SAY THAT COACHES JOH AND DAWSON ARE WONDERFUL.
WE'LL TALK MORE WITH THE COACHES ON PARENT NIGHT TOMORROW, BUT I'M PROUD OF YOU, KIDDO!
YOU'RE MAKING THE BEST OF AN UNFAIR SITUATION!

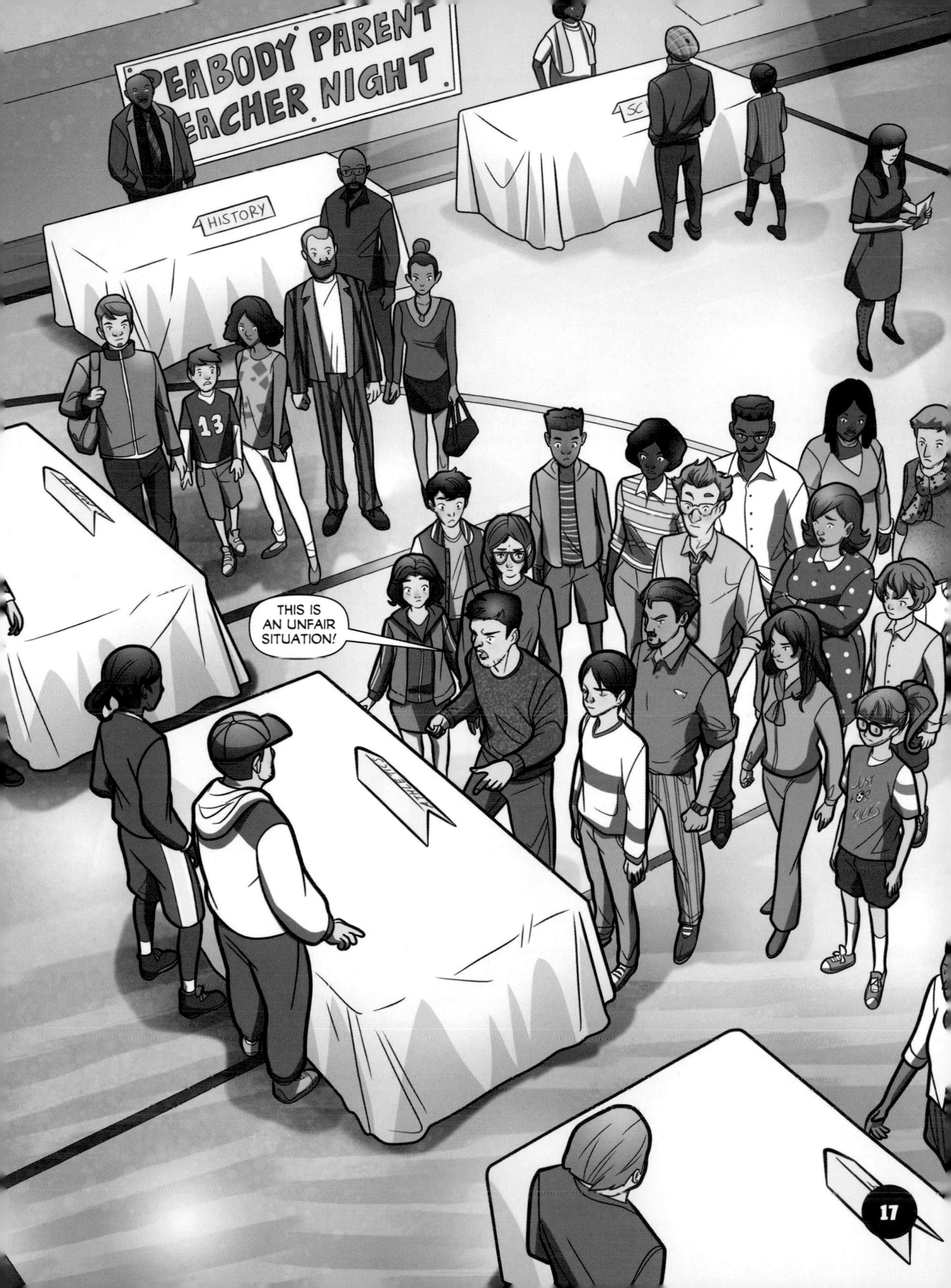
PEABODY PARENT TEACHER NIGHT
HISTORY
13
THIS IS AN UNFAIR SITUATION!
JUST FOR KICKS

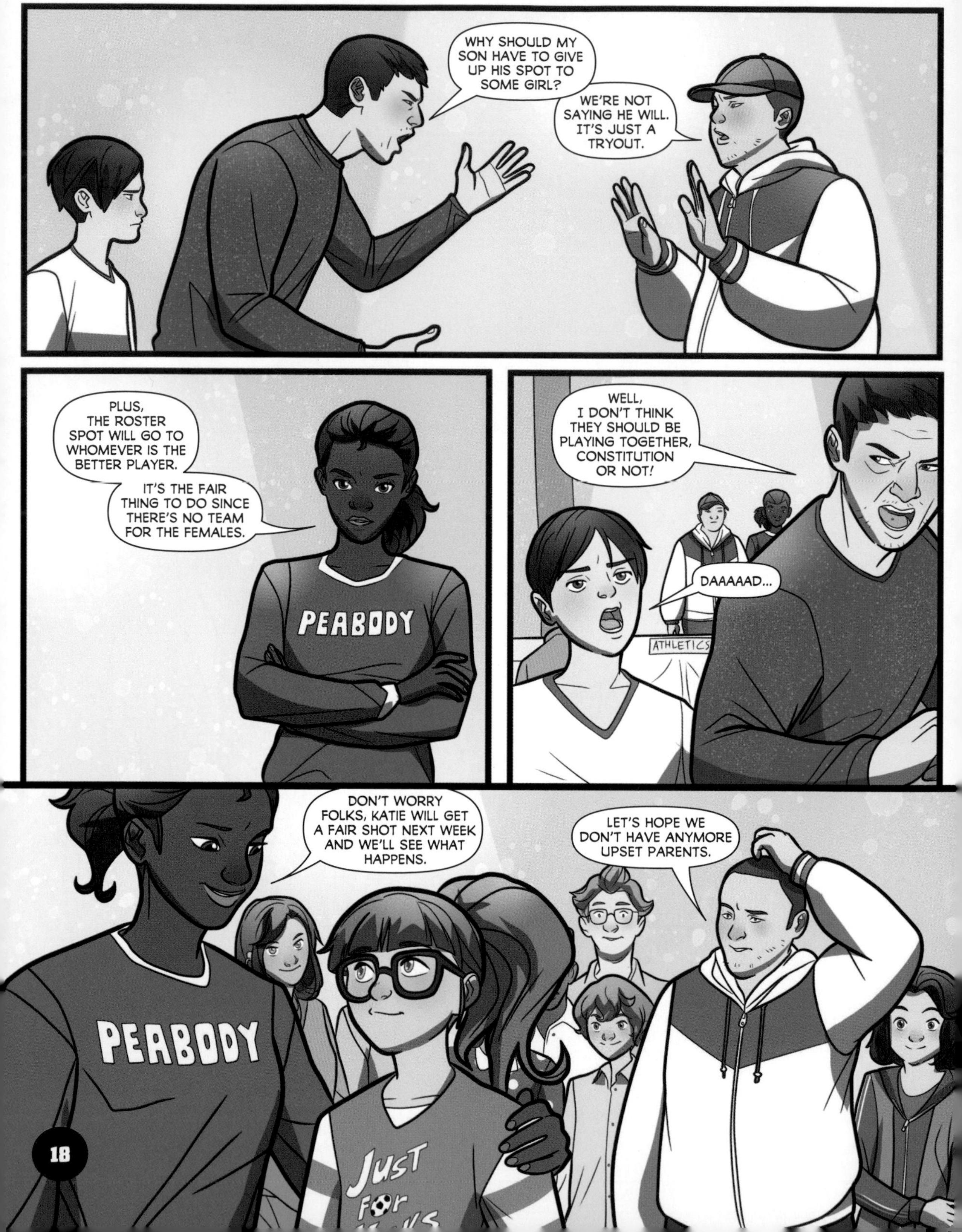
WHY SHOULD MY SON HAVE TO GIVE UP HIS SPOT TO SOME GIRL?
WE'RE NOT SAYING HE WILL. IT'S JUST A TRYOUT.
PLUS, THE ROSTER SPOT WILL GO TO WHOMEVER IS THE BETTER PLAYER.
IT'S THE FAIR THING TO DO SINCE THERE'S NO TEAM FOR THE FEMALES.
PEABODY
WELL, I DON'T THINK THEY SHOULD BE PLAYING TOGETHER, CONSTITUTION OR NOT!
DAAAAAD...
ATHLETICS
DON'T WORRY FOLKS, KATIE WILL GET A FAIR SHOT NEXT WEEK AND WE'LL SEE WHAT HAPPENS.
LET'S HOPE WE DON'T HAVE ANYMORE UPSET PARENTS.
PEABODY

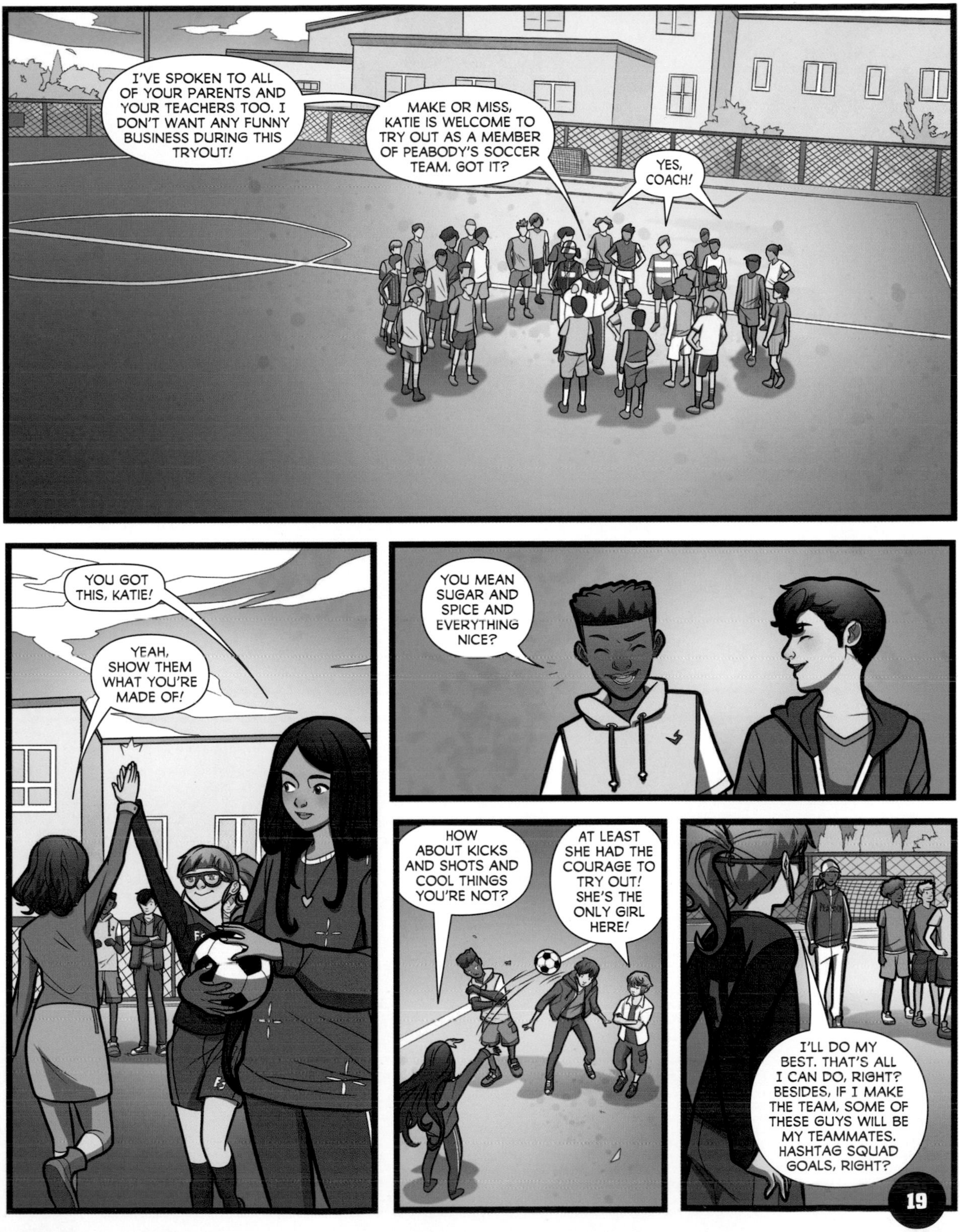
I'VE SPOKEN TO ALL OF YOUR PARENTS AND YOUR TEACHERS TOO. I DON'T WANT ANY FUNNY BUSINESS DURING THIS TRYOUT!
MAKE OR MISS, KATIE IS WELCOME TO TRY OUT AS A MEMBER OF PEABODY'S SOCCER TEAM. GOT IT?
YES, COACH!
YOU GOT THIS, KATIE!
YEAH, SHOW THEM WHAT YOU'RE MADE OF!
YOU MEAN SUGAR AND SPICE AND EVERYTHING NICE?
HOW ABOUT KICKS AND SHOTS AND COOL THINGS YOU'RE NOT?
AT LEAST SHE HAD THE COURAGE TO TRY OUT! SHE'S THE ONLY GIRL HERE!
I'LL DO MY BEST. THAT'S ALL I CAN DO, RIGHT? BESIDES, IF I MAKE THE TEAM, SOME OF THESE GUYS WILL BE MY TEAMMATES. HASHTAG SQUAD GOALS, RIGHT?

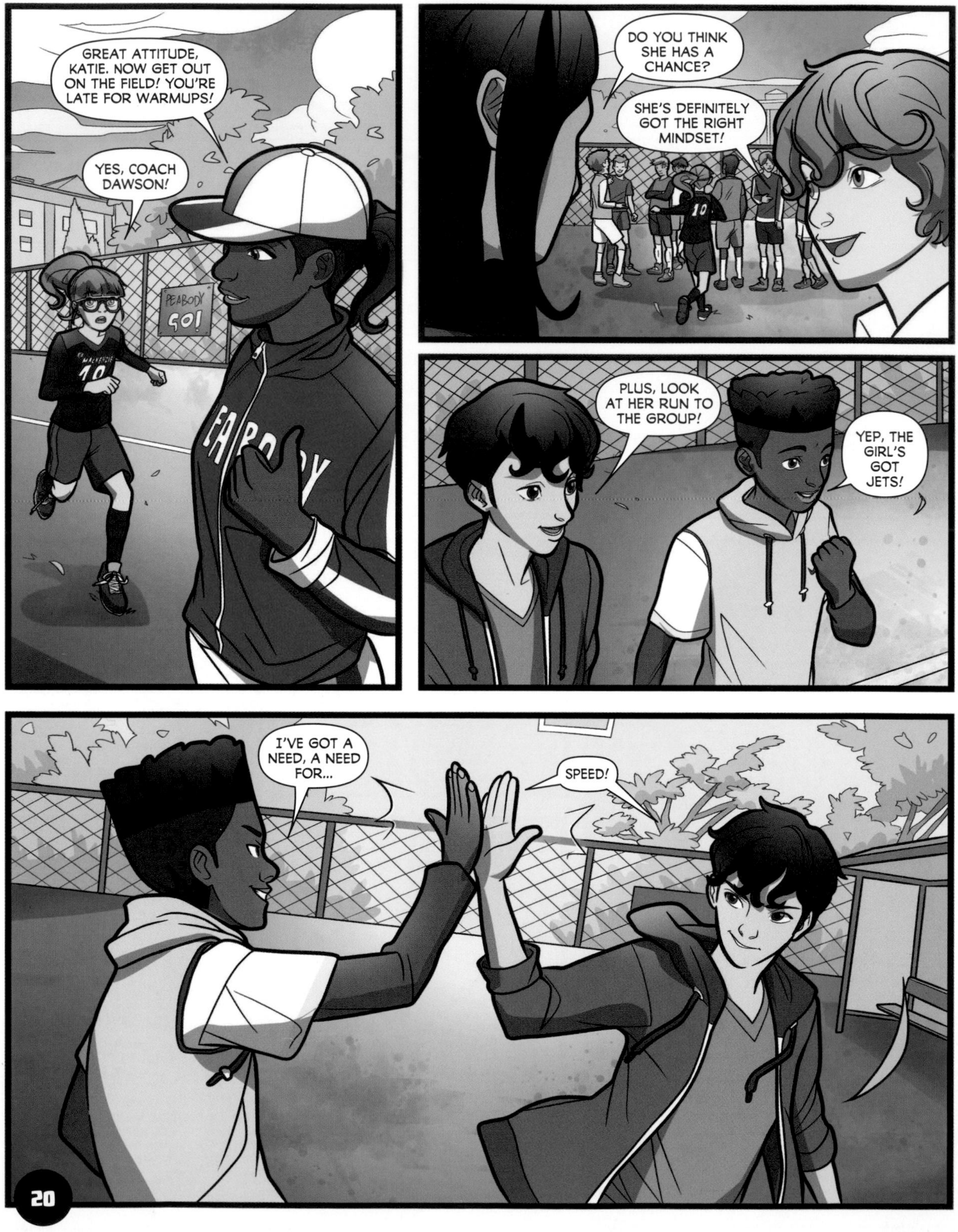
GREAT ATTITUDE, KATIE. NOW GET OUT ON THE FIELD! YOU'RE LATE FOR WARMUPS!
YES, COACH DAWSON!
PEABODY GO!
PEABODY
DO YOU THINK SHE HAS A CHANCE?
SHE'S DEFINITELY GOT THE RIGHT MINDSET!
PLUS, LOOK AT HER RUN TO THE GROUP!
YEP, THE GIRL'S GOT JETS!
I'VE GOT A NEED, A NEED FOR...
SPEED!

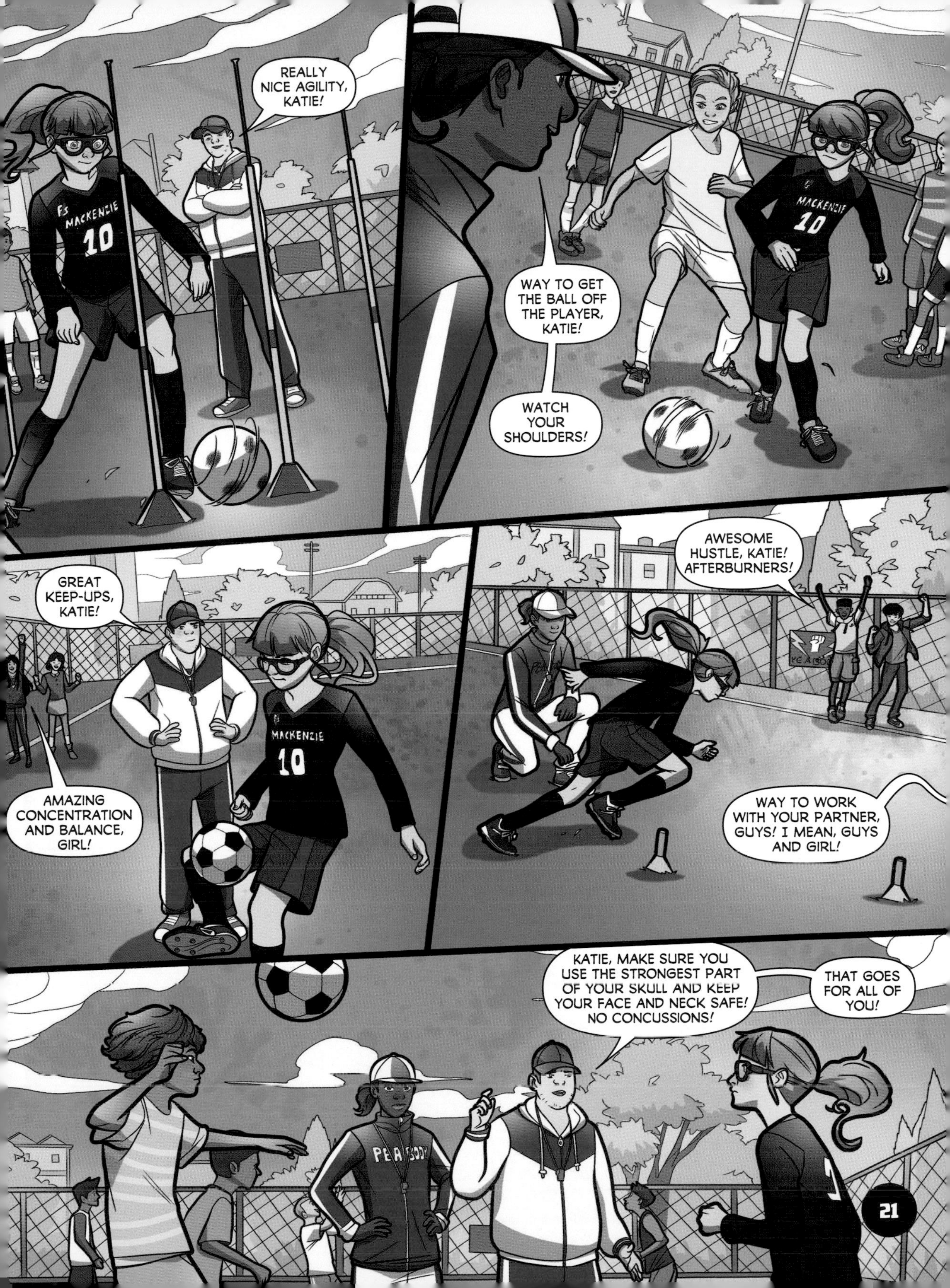

REALLY NICE AGILITY, KATIE!
MACKENZIE 10
WAY TO GET THE BALL OFF THE PLAYER, KATIE!
WATCH YOUR SHOULDERS!
GREAT KEEP-UPS, KATIE!
AMAZING CONCENTRATION AND BALANCE, GIRL!
AWESOME HUSTLE, KATIE! AFTERBURNERS!
WAY TO WORK WITH YOUR PARTNER, GUYS! I MEAN, GUYS AND GIRL!
KATIE, MAKE SURE YOU USE THE STRONGEST PART OF YOUR SKULL AND KEEP YOUR FACE AND NECK SAFE! NO CONCUSSIONS!
THAT GOES FOR ALL OF YOU!
PEABODY

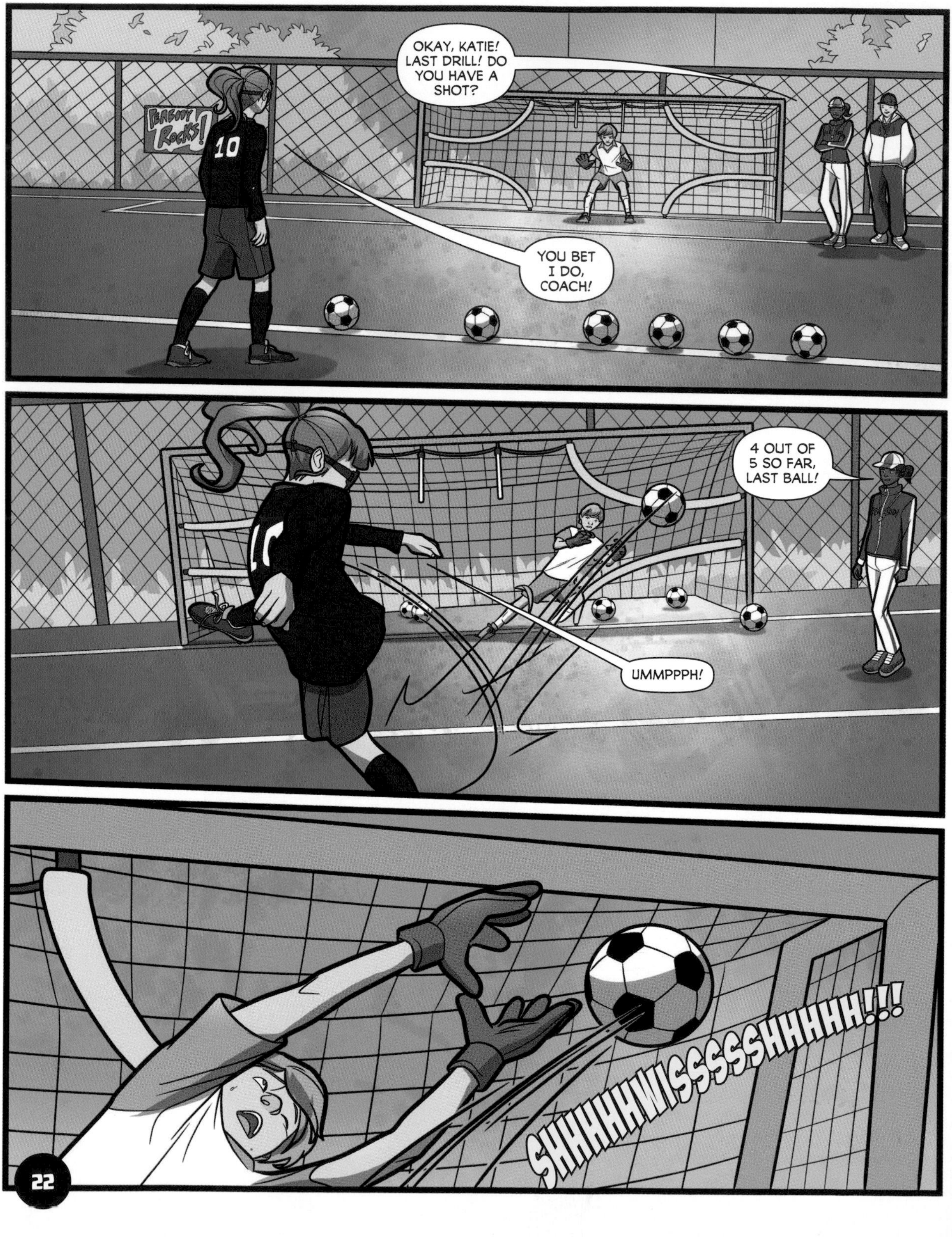

PEABODY ROCKS!
OKAY, KATIE! LAST DRILL! DO YOU HAVE A SHOT?
YOU BET I DO, COACH!
4 OUT OF 5 SO FAR, LAST BALL!
UMMPPPH!
SHHHHHWISSSSSSHHHHH!!!

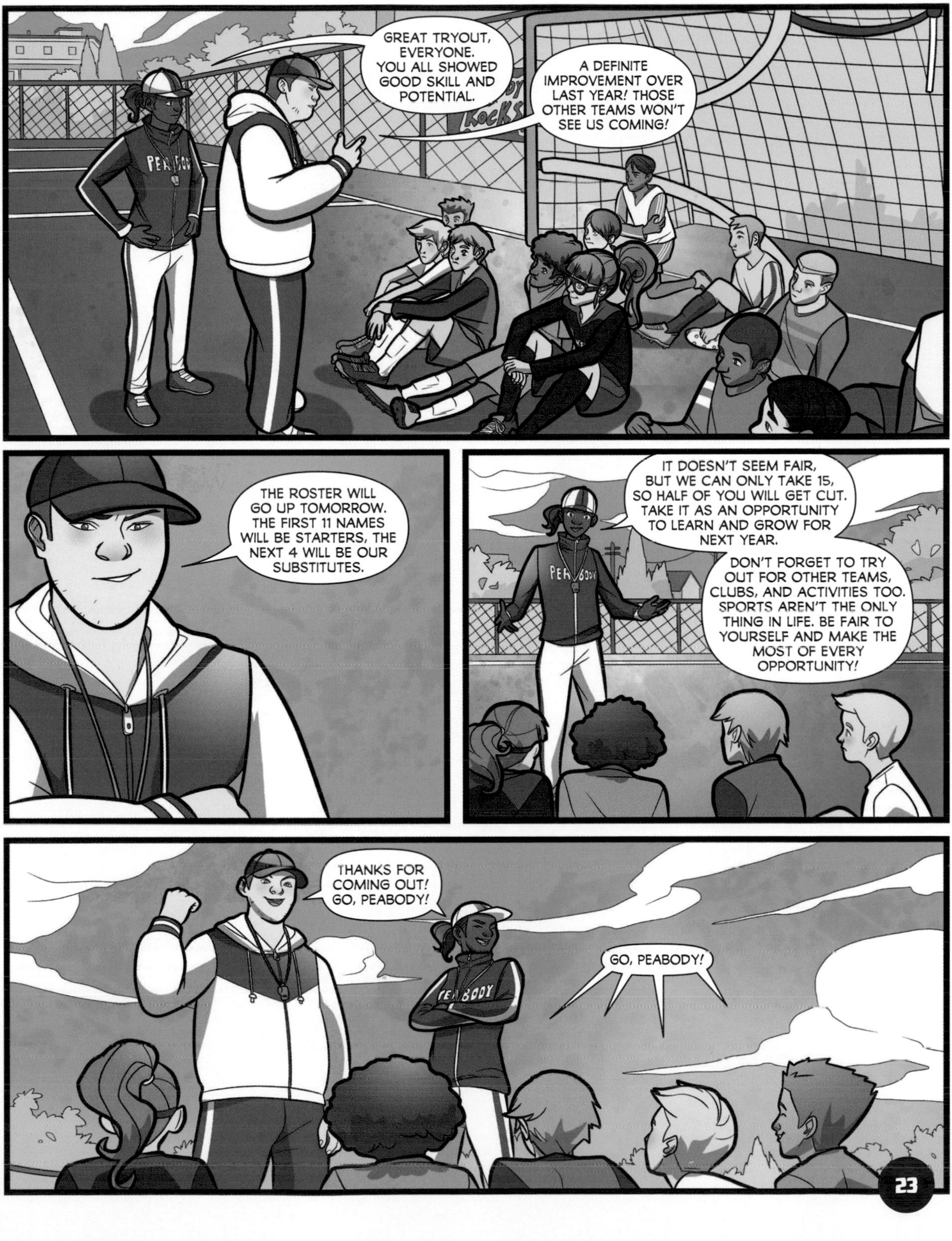
GREAT TRYOUT, EVERYONE. YOU ALL SHOWED GOOD SKILL AND POTENTIAL.
A DEFINITE IMPROVEMENT OVER LAST YEAR! THOSE OTHER TEAMS WON'T SEE US COMING!
THE ROSTER WILL GO UP TOMORROW. THE FIRST 11 NAMES WILL BE STARTERS, THE NEXT 4 WILL BE OUR SUBSTITUTES.
IT DOESN'T SEEM FAIR, BUT WE CAN ONLY TAKE 15, SO HALF OF YOU WILL GET CUT. TAKE IT AS AN OPPORTUNITY TO LEARN AND GROW FOR NEXT YEAR.
DON'T FORGET TO TRY OUT FOR OTHER TEAMS, CLUBS, AND ACTIVITIES TOO. SPORTS AREN'T THE ONLY THING IN LIFE. BE FAIR TO YOURSELF AND MAKE THE MOST OF EVERY OPPORTUNITY!
THANKS FOR COMING OUT! GO, PEABODY!
GO, PEABODY!

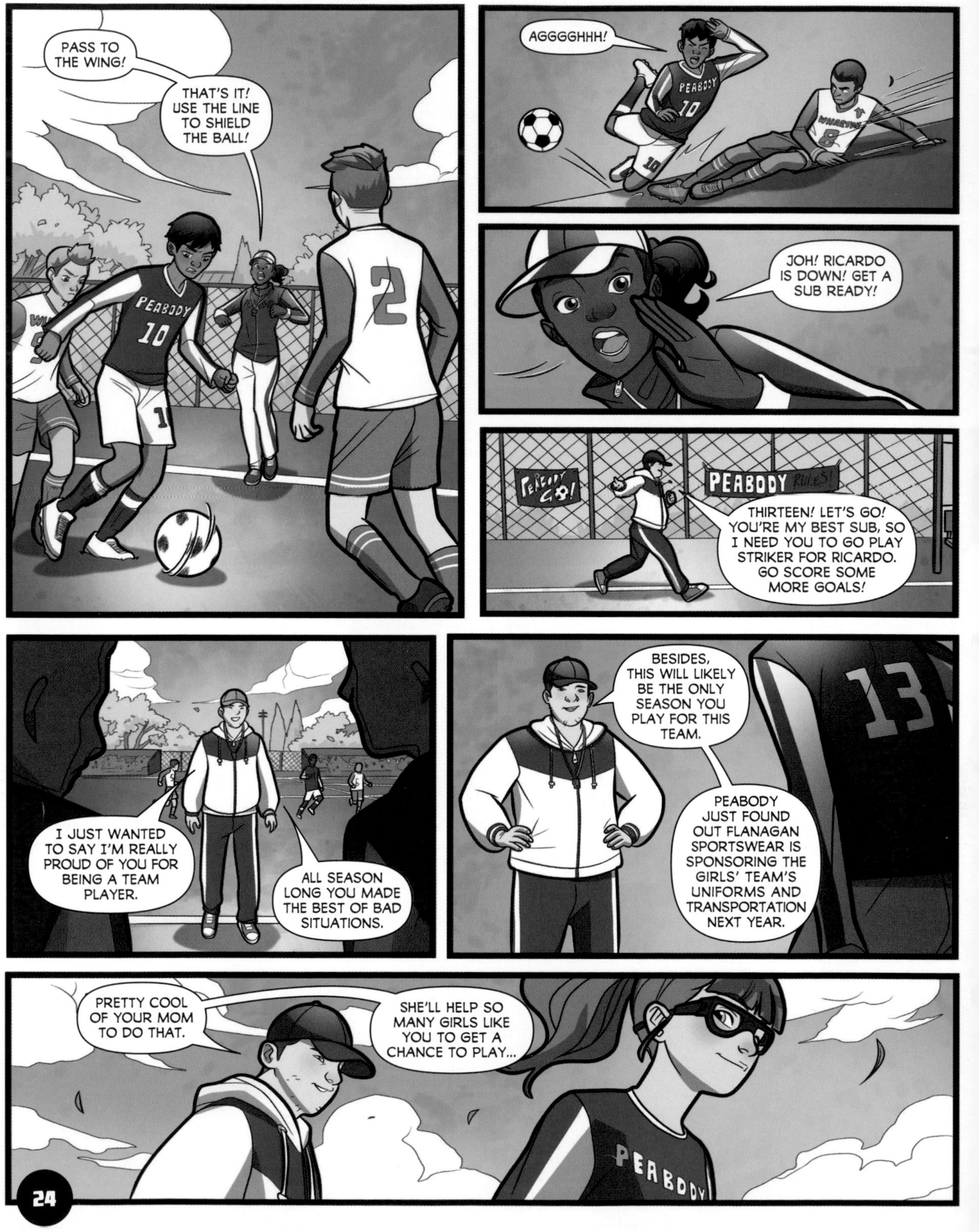
PASS TO THE WING!
THAT'S IT! USE THE LINE TO SHIELD THE BALL!
PEABODY 10
2
AGGGGHHH!
PEABODY 10
8
JOH! RICARDO IS DOWN! GET A SUB READY!
PEABODY GO!
PEABODY RULES!
THIRTEEN! LET'S GO! YOU'RE MY BEST SUB, SO I NEED YOU TO GO PLAY STRIKER FOR RICARDO. GO SCORE SOME MORE GOALS!
I JUST WANTED TO SAY I'M REALLY PROUD OF YOU FOR BEING A TEAM PLAYER.
ALL SEASON LONG YOU MADE THE BEST OF BAD SITUATIONS.
BESIDES, THIS WILL LIKELY BE THE ONLY SEASON YOU PLAY FOR THIS TEAM.
13
PEABODY JUST FOUND OUT FLANAGAN SPORTSWEAR IS SPONSORING THE GIRLS' TEAM'S UNIFORMS AND TRANSPORTATION NEXT YEAR.
PRETTY COOL OF YOUR MOM TO DO THAT.
SHE'LL HELP SO MANY GIRLS LIKE YOU TO GET A CHANCE TO PLAY...
PEABODY

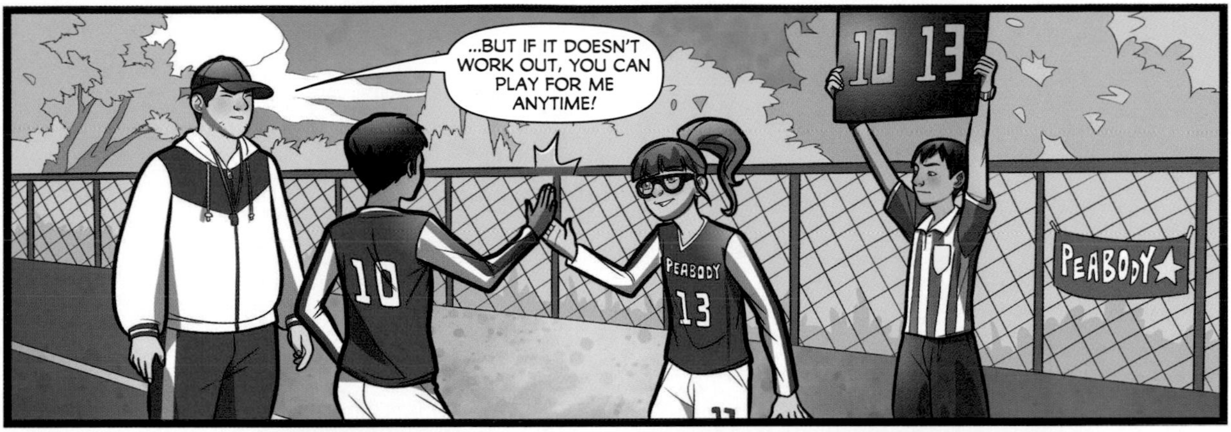
10 13
...BUT IF IT DOESN'T WORK OUT, YOU CAN PLAY FOR ME ANYTIME!
10
PEABODY
13
PEABODY★

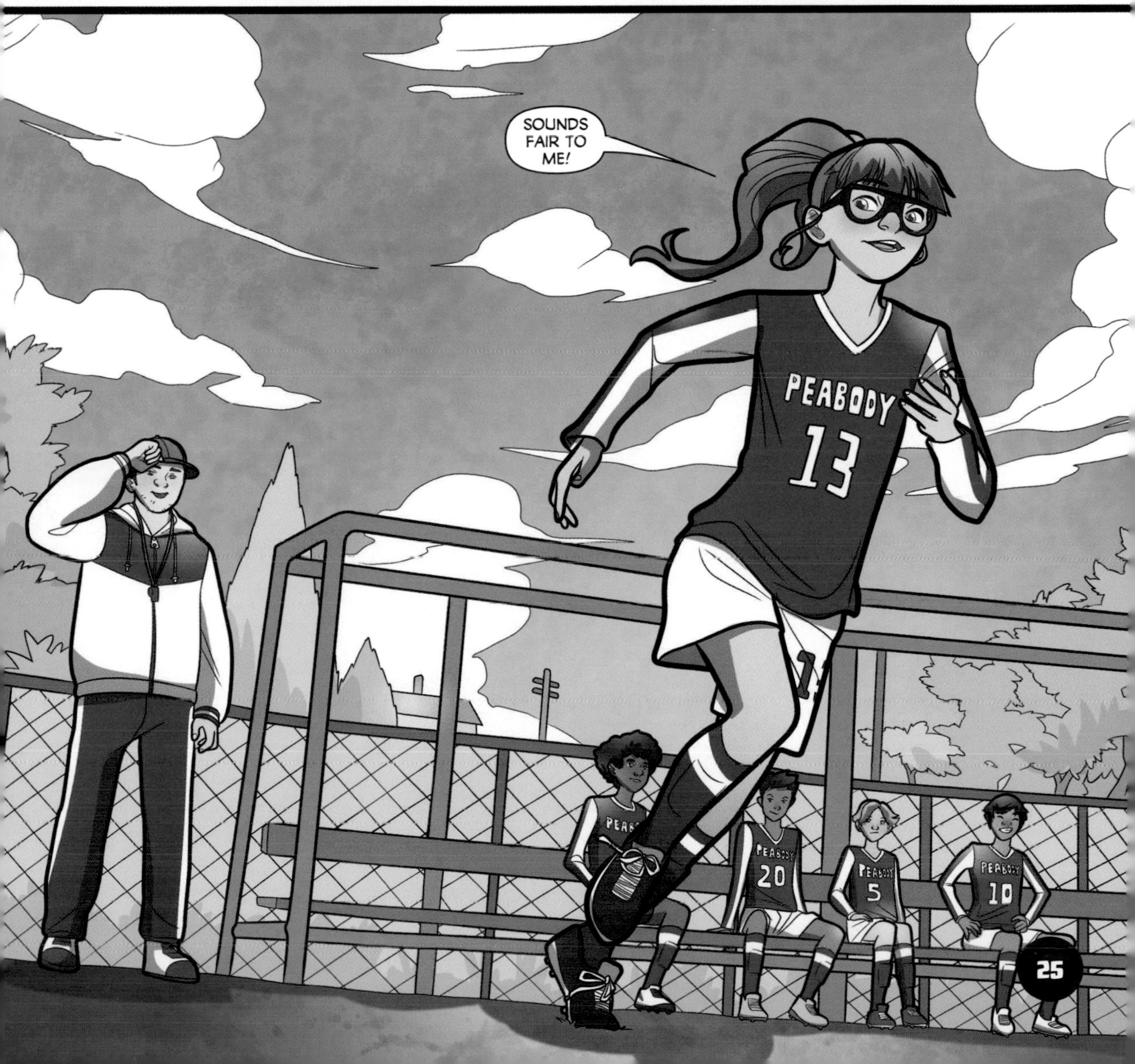
SOUNDS FAIR TO ME!
PEABODY
13
PEABODY
20
PEABODY
5
PEABODY
10

KATIE &

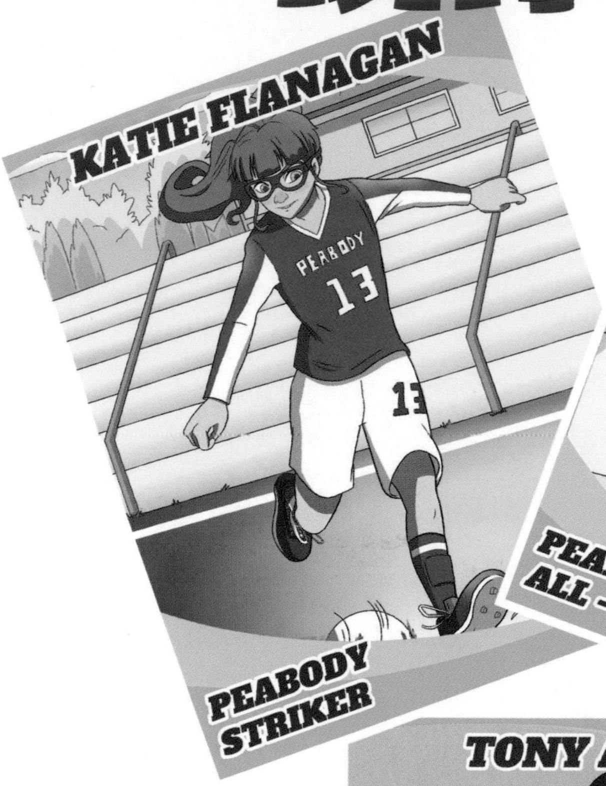
KATIE FLANAGAN
PEABODY
13
13
PEABODY
STRIKER

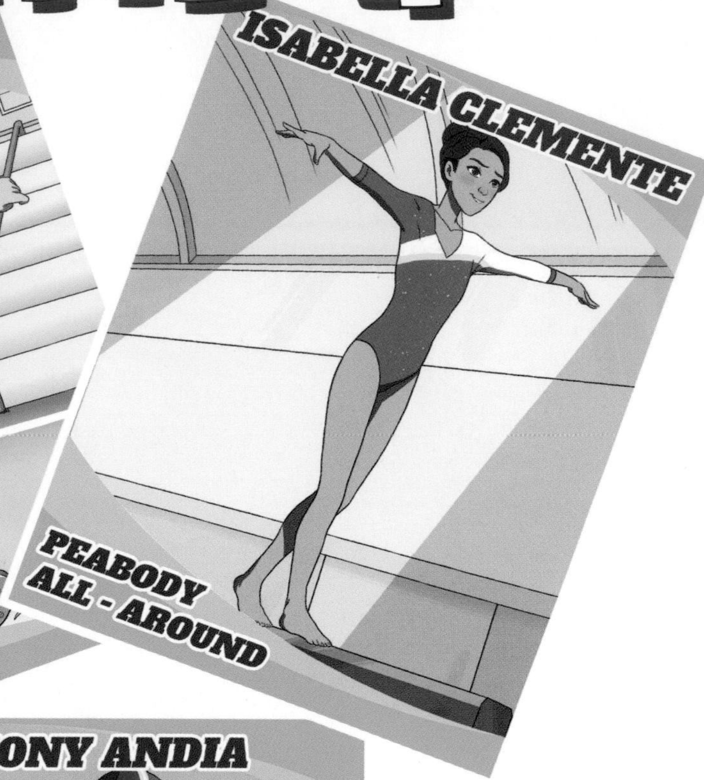
ISABELLA CLEMENTE
PEABODY
ALL - AROUND

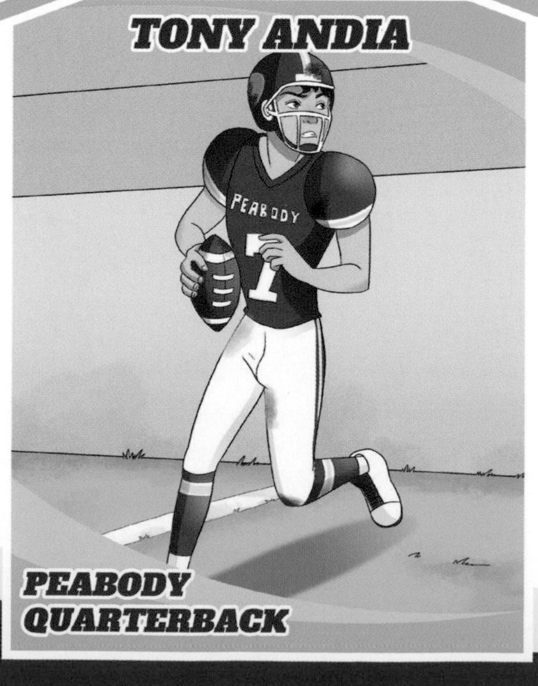
TONY ANDIA
PEABODY
7
PEABODY
QUARTERBACK

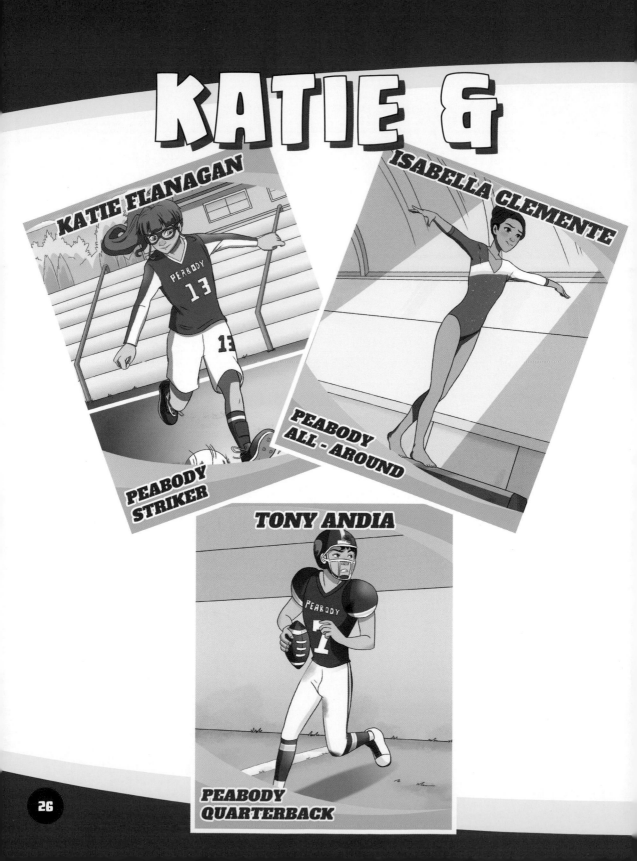

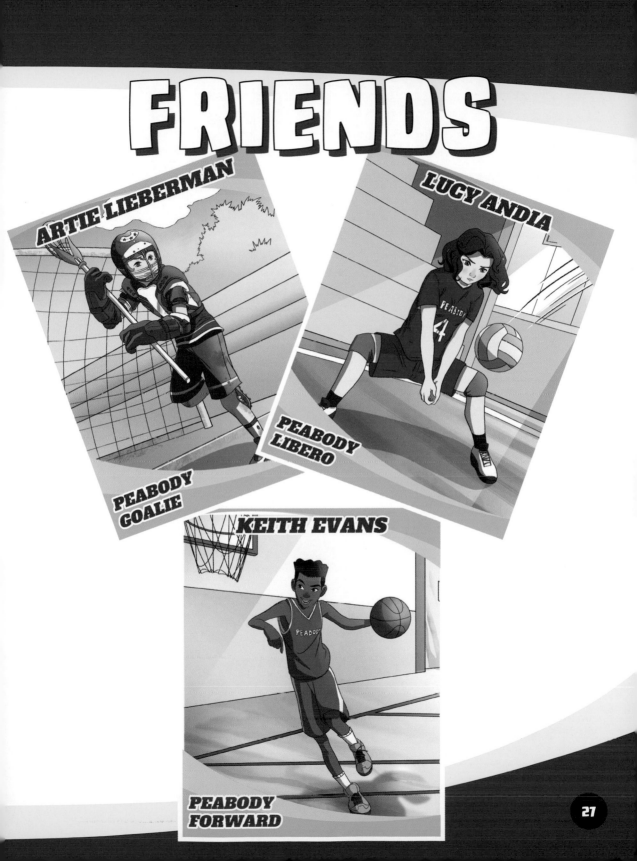

FRIENDS

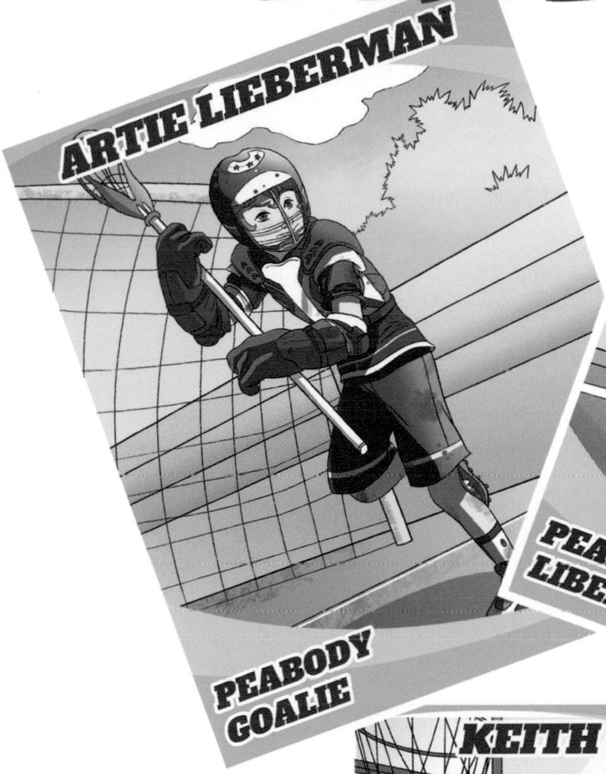
ARTIE LIEBERMAN
PEABODY
GOALIE

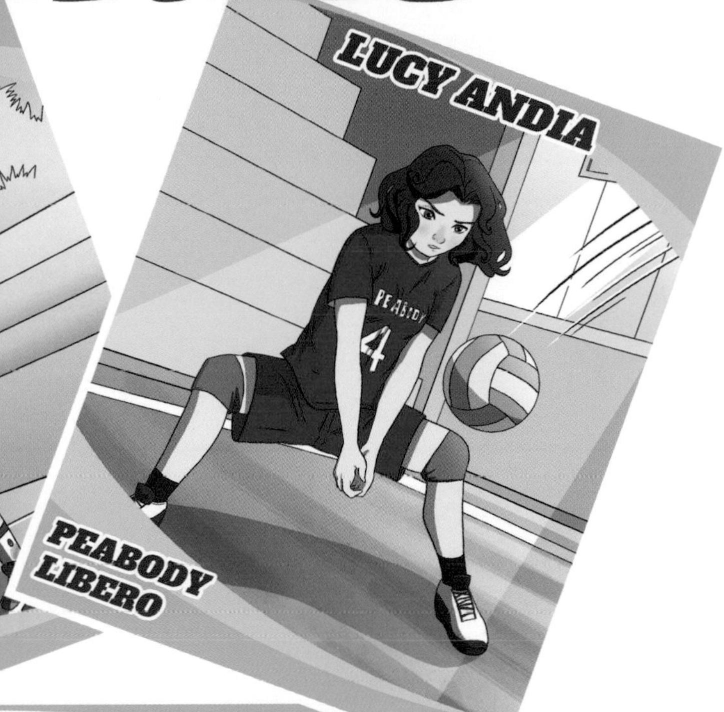
LUCY ANDIA
PEABODY
4
PEABODY
LIBERO

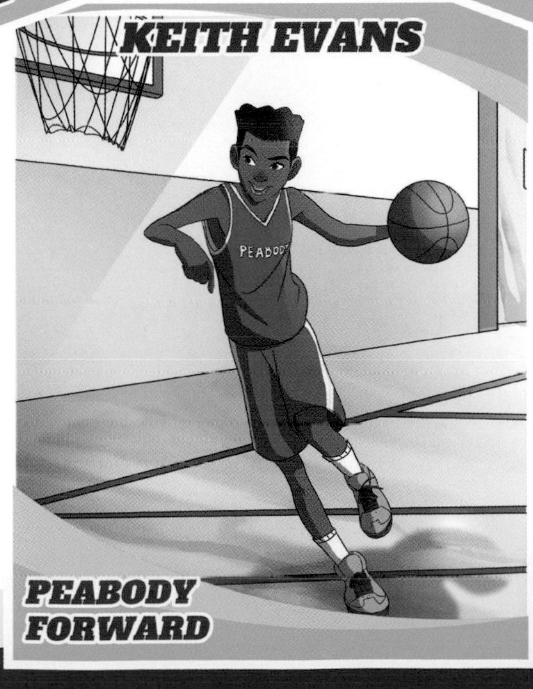
KEITH EVANS
PEABODY
PEABODY
FORWARD

SOCCER

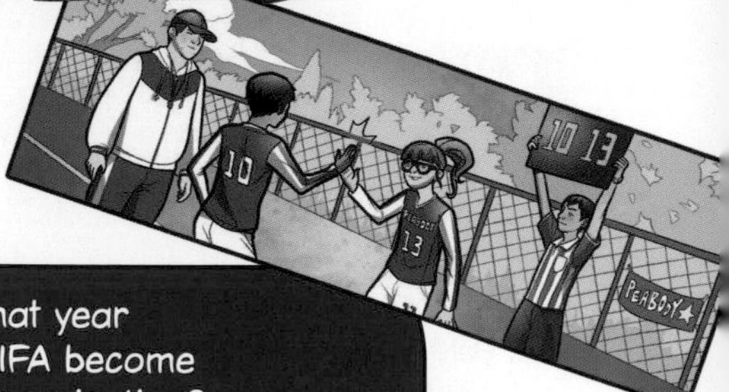
10 13
PEABODY

1. In most competitive leagues, how many players play per side in a regulation soccer match?

a. nine
b. ten
c. eleven
d. twelve

2. What year did FIFA become an organization?

a. 1704
b. 1804
c. 1904
d. 2004

3. What year was the first men's FIFA World Cup?

a. 1803
b. 1830
c. 1903
d. 1930

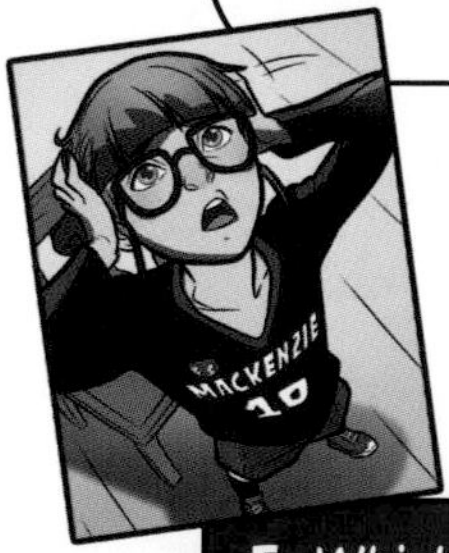
MACKENZIE

4. Who is the youngest American player to score a goal in MLS history at 14 years old?

a. Freddy Adu
b. Jozy Altidore
c. Michael Bradley
d. Landon Donovan

5. Which legendary female soccer player scored the winning shootout goal to help the United States earn a Women's World Cup title in 1999?

a. Brandi Chastain
b. Mia Hamm
c. Alex Morgan
d. Hope Solo

QUIZ

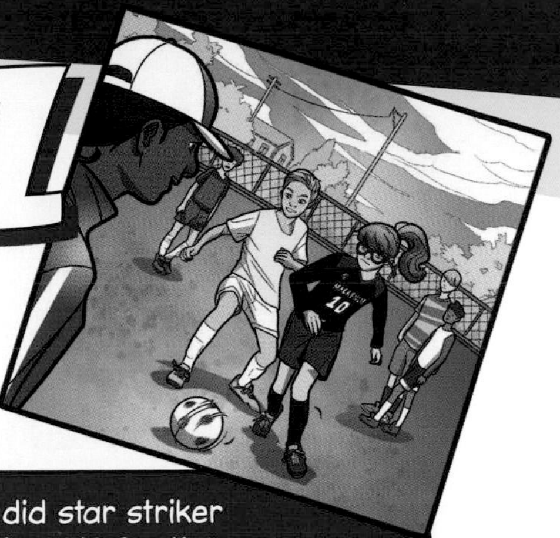

6. Which player has won the most men's FIFA World Cups with three trophies earned in four tournaments?

a. Cristiano Ronaldo
b. Lionel Messi
c. Pelé
d. Neymar

7. How many goals did star striker Alex Morgan score in 2012 for the United States women's national team?

a. 7
b. 14
c. 28
d. 35

8. Which Asian country shocked the world by defeating traditional European powerhouses Italy, Spain, and Portugal in the 2002 World Cup?

a. Japan
b. South Korea
c. Philippines
d. Taiwan

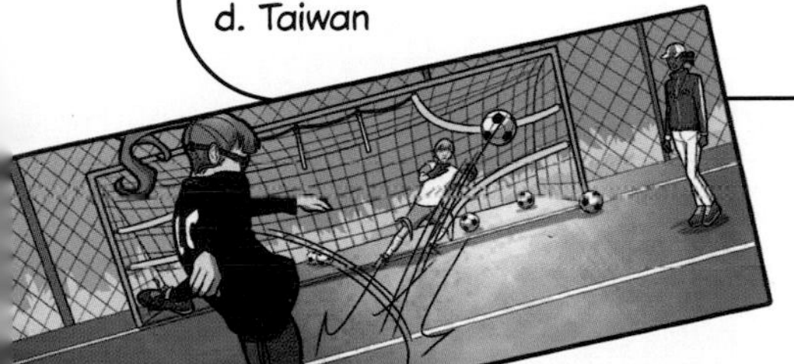

9. Which player is the all-time leading scorer in international soccer history with 184 goals?

a. David Beckham
b. Abby Wambach
c. Lionel Messi
d. Marta

10. Which player won two World Cups, two Olympic gold medals, played for her national team for 17 years and scored 158 international goals?

a. Marta, Brazil
b. Mia Hamm, United States
c. Christine Sinclair, Canada
d. Homare Sawa, Japan

* Answers on page 32

WHAT DO YOU THINK?

Fairness is often thought of as getting what you want, but it's really getting what is needed and what is just. However, true character is shown when you are able to positively respond to what might be seen as unfair in your personal situation.

 Describe a time when you thought you were being treated unfairly. How did you respond in that situation? Were you actually correct in your belief?

Katie didn't want to be thought of as a diva or star. Why do you think she believed that might not be fair to her teammates?

How did Katie's parents try to demonstrate responses to unfair life situations?

Why was a father upset with Katie being allowed to try out for the boys' team? Do you think the rule was fair? Why or why not?

Do you think it's fair that Katie should be asked to play on the girls' team in the future even if she's good enough to play amongst boys? Why or why not?

SOCCER FUN FACTS

1. The modern game of soccer originally started in 1863 as a variation of rugby football in England. Some historians believe "soccer" came about as a nickname for its formal name, "association football".

2. FIFA started with seven European nations as members, but now includes over 200 countries from around the world! Talk about growing the game!

3. Major League Soccer in North America began play in 1996. However, MLS was not the first professional US soccer league as the NASL existed between 1968 and 1984.

4. American soccer superstar Landon Donovan scored 144 MLS goals in his career. The MLS named its MVP trophy in honor of him!

5. Brazil has won the most men's World Cups with five (1958, 1962, 1970, 1994, and 2002). The United States has won the most women's World Cups with three (1991, 1999, and 2015).

GLOSSARY

agility – Ability to move and change direction quickly.

constitution – A set of rules for members of a group or organization to follow.

diva – Often referred to a skilled athlete or performer, but often seen as being egotistical and difficult to deal with due to a lack of humility or sportsmanship.

hat trick – Scoring three goals in one game, more common in hockey, where fans would throw their hats onto the ice in celebration after a player's third goal.

keeper – Short form for "goalkeeper."

scholarship – Earning free tuition to school because you are skilled in a specific area such as academics, athletics, and music.

squad – Team.

stoppage time – Time added at the end of each half in soccer to make up for time lost due to injuries, fouls, and substitutions.

striker – A position on a soccer team that is mainly focused on scoring goals instead of passing or defending.

ANSWERS

1. c   2. c   3. d   4. a   5. a   6. c   7. c   8. b   9. b   10. b

ONLINE RESOURCES

Booklinks
NONFICTION NETWORK
FREE! ONLINE NONFICTION RESOURCES

To learn more about soccer and fairness, visit **abdobooklinks.com**. These links are routinely monitored and updated to provide the most current information available.